Chasing Riffs

A Guitarist's Journey Through the 1980s and 1990s Rock Scene

By

SCOTT PATTERSON

ISBN: 979-8-9907112-6-6

"It's a Long Way to the Top
If You Want to Rock 'N' Roll"

AC/DC from the song "It's a Long Way to the Top"
From the album *T.N.T*
Written by Bon Scott, Malcolm Young, and Angus Young

The End

"So when is it your turn?" A voice sang behind me. I turned, beholding the most beautiful Latina I had ever seen. Her flowing black hair hung to her hips, perfectly framing her flawless face and exquisitely even dark complexion.

Her sparkling brown eyes stared seductively into mine. Her dazzling red dress hugged her body, and her large breasts desperately tried to break through their confinement to gasp a breath of fresh air.

"I'm sorry," I smiled, diverting my thoughts from what I wanted to do to her and thinking about the question she had asked instead. "But I'm not a dancer." I couldn't take my eyes off her chest and tried not to be obvious by staring into her eyes and using my peripheral vision to fulfill my fantasy. "I'm with the band."

"Well, you should be," she stated femininely, pushing her chest forward, emphasizing its size and drawing it closer. "I would love to show you mine if you want to show me yours," she whispered in my ear, pulling away and showing all she had to offer.

Thank you, God, I thought, stunned at her straightforwardness. I instantly fell in love with her and glanced at the male strippers jumping from the stage and making their way into the crowd. I drowned in her eyes, trying to say something witty, and felt as tongue-tied as a twelve-year-old boy asking a girl to his first dance.

She inched her way closer, hypnotizing me with her movements and tempting me with her lips. I put my hand on the small of her back and pulled her close, feeling her breasts press against my chest. The crowd disappeared, and time stood still as I dipped my head to touch her lips to mine.

A hand slapped me on the back, and I came to my senses, hearing the crowd and music again. I opened my eyes and twisted my neck to see who was behind me. My bass player, Damien, stood there smiling. At the same moment, my fantasy for the night was being interrupted by her friend in the same fashion Damien had interrupted me.

Damien had played bass with me almost since I arrived in Los Angeles. I was attending a music school and needed a place to stay. He and the drummer, Josh, were attending the same school and needed a roommate. Destiny was at play, and we had been a band ever since.

8

Damien's distraction was long enough for the girl's chaperone to grab her by the hand and pull her away. I tried to tighten my grip around her waist, but they disappeared into the crowd. "Show's about over, man." Damien's voice yelled in my ear. "It's about time to get tuned up."

He looked at the woman, turning her head to smile, and then at the stage behind him. "Come on, man. We've got about twenty minutes, and we can't be late again."

Late again. Last night was a drunken stupor for us all. It was a homecoming of sorts for Josh and Damien. We were ten minutes from their hometown, and the locals had shown up to support them and to get us drunk.

We played like shit, and by the end of the night, we could hardly crawl onto the stage, let alone be on time. The only thing that kept the bar owner happy was the size of the till at the end of the night.

I turned and slowly scanned the room full of women screaming and yelling at a man wearing a G-string and dancing in front of them. *She couldn't have gone far*, I thought, looking at the faces in the room, hoping to see her again. *I didn't even get her name.*

The women held dollar bills high as they rotated their hips in time with the music, whooping and hollering at the almost naked men gyrating in front of them. I watched the commotion, smiling in disbelief. I had never seen anything like this. These women were giving it their all, and the dancers were happy to respond in kind.

I loved being a musician. Seriously, do you think an accountant or cook at McDonald's would get attention from a girl like the one who just got away while they were working? Who in their right mind would settle for ordinary when they could have extraordinary?

Damien stepped up the stairs and onto the stage. He walked to his bass guitar, held the strap up, placed it over his head, and rested it on his shoulder. He plucked the top string, rotated the peg it was wound on, and ensured the pitch was correct.

I loved Damien. We clicked as soon as we met, and he could lay down a groove like no one I knew. He was the finest bass player I'd ever had the honor of creating music with. He was also the most remarkable person I've ever had the pleasure of knowing.

His jet-black hair hung to the middle of his back, and even though he had been losing weight since our endeavor began, he was still portly. His eyes were dark brown, and his high cheekbones gave him the look of a Native American.

I'm not sure if he actually descended from a tribe or if it was part of his heritage, but every time I looked at him, I envisioned him as a great Indian warrior or chief. It's funny how, with the time we spent together, we never got around to knowing personal details like that about each other.

It really didn't matter where we were from, who we descended from, how much money we had, or what we did in our lives. Music is the great unifier, and it doesn't discriminate. With music, we're all family. It's our common bond, our history. And that's why it's essential to our society.

The one thing I knew about Damien was that he was a seasoned bass player in both live performance and improvisation. We could get into a fucking train wreck and pull it off like it was written that way.

Having him on stage as part of the rhythm section was a pleasure. Having him as a friend was an honor. He took a lot of pressure off

10

me, and I trusted him with my life. He also had a calming effect that helped keep my demons away.

I walked up the stairs and looked over the crowd. I was still obsessing about the woman I'd been talking to earlier and hoped she'd stay and watch the show.

This club was one of the classier clubs we had played in our little circuit. The stage rose about three feet off the floor, and it had a second-story walkway where people could stand to watch the floor below or continue to a game room where they could play pool.

A few months ago, before Mark joined the band, Josh, Damien, and I watched Foghat play at this club. It was a privilege to be on the same stage they played on, but we weren't doing the venue any favors after our show last night.

In 1975, Foghat released the album "Fool For the City," and the title track was blasting on the airwaves. In 1977, they released *Foghat Live*, and the remake of the Big Joe Turner tune, "Honey Hush," helped shape my view of playing the guitar.

The Willie Dixon song "I Just Want to Make Love to You" spoke to me with its dual-guitar intro. It motivated me to teach Mark how to play guitar and to learn harmonies.

Foghat was one of the hottest bands on the airwaves when I was in high school, and our 8-track tape players would blast them in our cars as we cruised up and down Main Street. When I was a kid fantasizing about being a rock star, this was one of the bands I fantasized about doing it with.

I'd been to a couple of their concerts with audiences of fifty thousand plus, and I know they played in larger venues in other cities. Watching this icon of my time perform at this small club, which probably held around 300 people, was unsettling. I wondered how it felt knowing you once sold out huge auditoriums and then ended up playing a shithole like this.

Yeah, I know I said it was one of the classier clubs we'd played, but it was still a neighborhood bar. Whether you're an original band, a copy band, or a cover band, if you're playing in a bar, your job is to sell drinks, not albums. Selling drinks makes a bar owner rich. Selling albums makes the band rich. It had to be humbling to be in a bar selling drinks when you once played arenas and sold millions of records.

I played more of these beer-stained disasters than Foghat knew existed. This one was just like all the others. Filled with the same faces and the same stories. The good news here was we didn't have to move pool tables off the dance floor, and we didn't, thank God, have to haul all this shit up a flight or more of stairs. Everything has a "Touch of Gray" or a silver lining if you look hard enough.

I walked over to my Marshall half-stack amplifier and picked up one of my guitars, which was sitting on a stand beside it. "Here's the song list for tonight." Mark, the singer, and my little brother yelled in my ear while handing me a copy of the list he just made.

I grabbed it and set it on top of my amp. The red lights on my tuner reached the middle of the meter, turning green, showing the string was in pitch. My stomach grew queasy as I continued this ritual with each of the strings. Satisfied that this guitar was in tune, I unstrapped it, set it on the stand, and picked up the set list.

I gave the list a once-over before grabbing another guitar and tuning it. "This won't work," I yelled as I set down my gold-top Les

Paul and walked towards Mark, who was staring at his guitar tuner, ensuring our sounds matched.

"What?"

"I said that this won't work, man." I handed him back the paper and stood silent as he re-read it.

"What do you mean it won't work? It's the song list for the first set." He returned it to me and turned his attention back to his tuner.

"No shit?! Now, come on, Mark, we just sat through a male strip show that could be the most incredible thing I've ever seen. These women were getting away with anything they wanted. And they wanted a lot. Now look out there, man."

I raised my arm, sweeping the room with it, trying to make a point, and spotted the woman I'd been talking to earlier. I hesitated while watching her smile and move her fingers up and down, giving me a sexy wave.

I wanted her so badly I could feel my loins warming. I had a quick thought of jumping off the stage and banging her right there in front of God and everybody, and regained my senses by looking at Mark and the set list in my hand.

"There's a room full of horny women who are dying to do the fucking bump and grind, Mark," I yelled over the noise, still watching the lady in red and feeling my jeans tighten from the fantasy in my mind. "You can't open with AC/DC and the Scorpions. Let's pull out some Journey and other mellow shit that we know so they can do their thing."

"No way, man. They'll enjoy these tunes just as much as the others, and plenty of guys will be here soon. This'll work, man, I guarantee it."

"Look, Mark." I stared into his eyes and then moved my gaze to my cosmic connection. "We're not playing to a bunch of your adolescent fucking friends, and if you would open your fucking eyes and look around, you would see that. Look around, Mark, and tell me, would you rather be down there bumping and grinding, or would you rather be listening to a hard, upbeat song, looking at all the girls trying to get up the courage to scream in their ear and ask if they want to dance? Let's let them fucking bump and grind."

I turned and walked away, listening to him scream about how I wasn't always able to get my way just because I was the oldest, blah blah blah. I jumped off the stage and walked towards our table. I looked where my encounter of fate had been standing, and she had vanished. *Fuck*, I thought, *now where did she go?*

Mark was my brother, and I loved him, but he had a lot to learn about audiences. I detoured and ducked into the bathroom, hiding in a stall and pulling a folded paper from my top pocket. My stomach twisted, and I lifted the toilet seat, emptying its contents into the waiting water below. This had been going on for years, and I didn't know how to stop it. Every night, when it was about time to take the stage, I would get violently ill.

While some people get butterflies in their stomachs, I got pterodactyls in mine. When the first song started, they would fly away, and I would be fine. It was weird, and I learned early not to get on my knees in these piss-stained, shit-smelling rooms.

Other than the nasty bar bathroom smell and the piss on the floor, throwing up was something I had gotten used to. After the heaving stopped, a line of cocaine always re-energized and refocused me for the night.

Mark's father left before he was born. I was seven, and it wasn't the first of Mom's relationships I witnessed end. My father had left almost three years earlier. Each time, I watched as she drank, sobbed, cried, and stayed in her room for what seemed like weeks. If she wasn't in her room, she was screaming at me about how I was a horrible child who couldn't take care of his brother.

As she escaped her misery, people would parade in and out of our house as she drank, drugged, and fucked away her problems. When I started junior high school, Mark was almost three. Ken came into our lives, and we made a family.

Mark started junior high school when I was nineteen. I was busy living in a band house, getting laid, having my first taste of blow, and enjoying the riches that come from being a rock star. I didn't want anyone wondering about my perpetually plugged or runny nose, so I started using Afrin nasal spray.

As busy as I was, I still found time to pick up Mark occasionally. We would go fishing or do some other activity on a Saturday or Sunday afternoon, with me sneaking off anywhere I could to do a line and spray the snot-reducing elixir, Afrin, in my nose.

I wiped my mouth with toilet paper hanging on a roll from the interior wall and pulled a small mirror from my pocket. I placed it on the back of the toilet and carefully unfolded a rectangular paper, exposing a fine white powder.

I tapped a small amount of the powder on the mirror and cut it up with my driver's license. I pulled a dollar bill from my pocket and rolled it up, making a straw.

I always thought that being paid for what you love to do was the ultimate way to live. It never occurred to me that when it became a way of paying bills, it became just another monotonous job.

Every gig was a learning experience, but it also brought us one step closer to closing the doors on other employment opportunities. Playing in a band was an occupational choice that was hard to change. Playing in a cover band was a way of closing the doors I had dreamed about opening.

I snorted a line of the white powder through each nostril and pinched my nose. I let go of it, sniffing as hard as possible, and wiped the end of my nose with my thumb and forefinger. My stomach settled, and my energy levels rose, giving me the confidence to get on stage and play.

Mark joined the choir when he entered junior high school, and his voice garnered him a lot of attention. Mom couldn't have been prouder. A couple of years later, I gave him extra confidence by accompanying him on an acoustic ballad we had written for his school's talent show.

Honestly, I did it more for me than for him, but the girls went wild, and the boys wanted to be his friend. Popularity wasn't something I had ever known, and I have to admit I was a little jealous, but happy he got to experience it.

He quickly gravitated to the latchkey kids, who had no particular time to be home, and followed in my footsteps. He wasn't getting in trouble, necessarily, but he might have been drinking and even drugging a little. Mom thought otherwise, and her protective behavior increasingly kept him away from home.

I promised her I would spend more time with him and see if I could get him back on the "right track." Ken became Mom's longest and steadiest relationship ever. They both worked long hours, so quality parenting time wasn't something either of us experienced.

It wasn't long before I found out Mark hated Ken. He never explained why, but he avoided any conversations that mentioned Ken's name. If I asked him about his home life, he either gave me a blank stare or said, "I don't want to talk about it." It was apparent why he didn't want to go home for days at a time, but I didn't want to be the one to tell Mom.

He wanted me to ask him to move in with me, but I couldn't expose him to the band house scene I was living in. At least not yet. I think his resentment of me grew because of it. Mom and Ken had a decent middle-class life, and even though Mark hated Ken, I thought he was better off with them than he was with me.

The following year, I was learning to navigate the club scene in one of the "funnest" bands in the city. Even though we played other bands' music, I dreamed of being "signed."

I've always loathed the thought of being ordinary, and rock stars were anything but ordinary. Getting to know people in the local scene was an excellent way to start, and it gave me a feeling of being extraordinary, if only in a small way. Plus, I really needed the money.

I licked the mirror clean and pushed open the stall door, walking to the sink and looking in the mirror hanging above it. I lifted my head, checking the inside of my nose. Satisfied there were no cocaine boulders lodged inside, I turned on the water, filled my cupped hand, and swished the water in my mouth, spitting it into the sink. I put my wet fingers in my nose and sniffed the moisture as I pulled them out.

I hated throwing up every night before a gig. I hated the taste in my mouth after throwing up. I hated the shit smell in these fucking excrement receptacles, and I hated the dependency I'd developed on Afrin. I pulled on the bathroom door and was back in the crowd.

I sucked air deep and fast through my nose, breathing in the smoke-filled "clean air" and making sure nothing had slipped out of my nasal cavity. I pinched my nose again and looked around the bar for the lady in red with renewed vigor.

Musically, our band couldn't be touched. I discovered Mark could sing when he was young, around nine or ten. Before he went to junior high school and before he joined the choir. I was still in high school, and with times being what they were, we shared a room.

Van Halen released their self-titled debut album a year earlier, and it changed how guitar players played guitar forever. Only a few players have accomplished that feat. Eddie Van Halen was one, Jimi Hendrix was another, and Link Wray, the first player to push a screwdriver through his speaker to achieve that distorted sound, was a third.

I sat and listened to Van Halen's debut album all night, every night, for the first week. Then, I spent the next three years trying to learn the awe-inspiring sounds emanating from the vinyl disc.

One night, I was doing my thing, learning some licks, when Mark walked in. I think I was trying to learn "Atomic Punk" or "On Fire." Hell, I might have even been taking a break and listening to "Ice Cream Man" out of frustration.

When he walked in, he started singing. Even though he sang in a low, embarrassed voice, he sounded pretty good and could keep a steady pitch. He hadn't hit puberty yet, and it was the first time I saw

18

him take an interest in anything, so I began teaching him what little music knowledge I had.

When I first started learning guitar, I ran scales up and down the neck. If I wanted to learn a song, I would sit with a record player and move the needle back and forth until I wore out the grooves. If I were going to a friend's house to jam, it was to lay down a I-IV-V chord progression and figure out variations of the chords and the scale patterns that worked over those chords.

In my opinion, it was the grooviest part of playing. I loved laying down a progression and improvising leads on top of it more than anything. To this day, when we're playing live, and there's only a waitress and a bartender in the audience, I'll intentionally cause train wrecks in songs.

It allows the band to deviate from the covers and empowers me to stretch my limits. I know it's not the proper way to play in a cover band, but I can't help it. Improvisation is my drug of choice. I had been addicted to it since I started playing, and I would chase it throughout my entire career.

When Mark and I practiced, I tried to instill the same principles of improv into him. In order to break the rules, you first need to know the rules. So, I would make him run scales with his voice while I played them on the guitar.

Then, we would work on learning an additional part of a song or writing an original. Even then, I knew originals were the only way to make money in this profession, and a few of ours sounded pretty good.

A few years after I started working with Mark on singing, I graduated from high school and started working in a music store.

Months after that, I moved into the band house and started playing with my first garage band, which also played cover songs. I know Mark felt abandoned when I left. He couldn't understand why I wasn't still living at home, and I know he felt resentment when I didn't ask him to move in with me.

When puberty finally took hold of Mark, it affected his voice. He couldn't hit the same highs he once did, but his voice still had a unique "star" quality, and I hoped he would develop it while I was figuring out who I was.

About a year later, when I was in my first working band, Mark and I wrote our last original song together. It was for his talent show. We drifted apart after that and did little together musically. The originals we worked on sat in a drawer until they seemed forgotten.

I had my band and career to deal with. Mark had school and formed his own group. They played in our garage and followed the same path I had forged years before. He never asked for advice or help with his new band, and I never thought to offer any.

After two years of practice, they started playing at school parties and dances. Mark's singing was the talk of the town, and he was getting more attention and girls than I ever did at his age.

I was proud of his accomplishments. He had something to prove and was determined to do it without my help. The only time I tried to talk to him about it, I received a blank stare and a smile.

When I started teaching him, I told him that the most important thing as a vocalist was to have his own sound system. One that was big enough to fill a club.

I'll be damned if he didn't listen and save up his money for what must have been years so he could put it all down on the PA we were using now. He had developed into an unbelievable singer, with the attitude and rage to match.

When I went for my first audition for the "funnest" band in the city, I realized I could make money, drink beer, and get laid by playing popular music of the day in local clubs. I jumped in with both feet and saw ordinary as well as Mark being left behind.

Learning that you can make money playing other people's music is a trap. Money was always an issue for our family, and playing in a cover band was a way to help make ends meet. I think that's why most musicians play in cover bands.

Let's face it, there are only two types of musicians in the world. The rich "A musicians" who make it big by getting signed to a record deal and pump out top-ten hits. And the poor "B musicians" who play for fifty to a hundred dollars a night and struggle, never having enough to survive.

When Mark moved to LA and joined the band, our collaborations picked up where they had left off. They were more refined, more professional, and more promising. As a band, we began putting together originals, and the possibility of being signed was more palpable than ever. After what seemed like a lifetime of playing dive bars, there was light at the end of the tunnel.

Unfortunately, the real world was looming in front of us, and learning forty songs, hauling equipment around, and working full-time jobs to pay the bills drained our minds, bodies, and souls. Originals were once again put on hold, and tonight was about paying for our room, our gas, and our supply of cigarettes, alcohol, and drugs.

Mark and I were brothers. I wish I could say we could read each other's minds and breathe in time with one another, but we couldn't. His feelings of abandonment and anger towards me hadn't dissipated over the years; it had gotten worse. He now had this need to prove he was better than me, and I still thought something was off with him, just like I did when we brought him home.

I attended the Guitar Institute of Technology in Hollywood, California. It was a one-year school that allowed me to play and learn from talented players from around the world. When I graduated, Mark's band broke up, his girlfriend left him, and he was in trouble with the law again. It sounded like a bad country song, but I talked to Mom, and after some stern conversations, we agreed it would be best if he moved to Los Angeles with me.

After a series of unfortunate events during a gig with a singer we met at school, we needed a singer. We were all working "real jobs" to pay the bills, and when I explained the situation to Damien and Josh, they didn't have a problem with him moving in as long as he could pull his weight and ease some of our financial burdens.

Mark was a scrawny twenty-year-old when he arrived. He believed Hollywood would find him and that all his dreams would come true. We didn't want to be the ones to burst his bubble, but you should have seen his face the first time we took him out on the town.

We went to the Roxy, the Troubadour, and then to a couple of dive bars where bands like ours played. He got a lesson in humility that night when he heard some of the monster singers and players who inhabited these clubs. I think it broke his dream and brought him back to reality, but honestly, with his attitude, it was needed.

It was inevitable that he would be here. We were brothers. I had worked with him during his most formative years, and our harmonies fit together like no other. All he needed, I always felt, was the maturity he gained while I was away.

The goal of attending the Guitar Institute was not to get good but to become extraordinary. I wanted to be a force to be reckoned with on guitar. I knew that with my chops and Mark's voice, we couldn't be beat.

We gave Mark a crash course in learning forty songs, and in two weeks, we were off, playing parties in the Los Angeles area, "proving" ourselves. When our manager gave us the opportunity to play in clubs up and down the San Joaquin Valley, we jumped at it.

This was our fifth stop since we had left Los Angeles. In two weeks, we would be in Sacramento, and then we would make our way back through these same clubs, adding a couple of new ones as we completed the loop and headed back to our home base of Los Angeles.

I reached our table and sat down, grabbing my drink with one hand and pulling a cigarette from the pack sitting next to the drink with the other. Damien sat with his long-term girlfriend at the next table, and Josh, the drummer, sat with his new special friend next to them.

I pulled a lighter from my pocket and was lighting my cigarette when I spied the lady I had fallen in love with earlier. She smiled seductively and squeezed her tits almost out of her dress as she bent down to talk to some guy at a table. *God, I want her,* I thought as I quickly rearranged Mark's set list.

Mark took the three-foot jump from the stage and landed on the dance floor. He resented and was angry with me, but he looked up to me and saw me as an adult. He always had. The thing he hated most was my authority.

He didn't like me leading the band, being older than him, or that Damien, Josh, and I were so close. Only time could create the bond that would catapult us to stardom, and I understood that. I was biding my time and taking it one step at a time.

I could still see the resentment building in his eyes from our argument over the set list. Something had seemed off with him since Bakersfield, and he wasn't going to let this go. He'd been sleeping a lot, and I chalked it up to exhaustion from the trip. I distributed the new list to Josh and Damien.

"Hey, Mark," I yelled, walking towards him and handing him a copy of the new set list. "I'm sorry about getting upset earlier. We're brothers, and as family, we really need to work together." I stepped closer and looked into his eyes. "Come on, Mark, I gave you the name. And you know how much I hate that fucking name."

He smiled, and I slapped my hand on his back. We shook the bro shake. "You know it's too bad," he whispered in my ear. "We really had something that was working."

I smiled and turned. The meaning didn't register until I reached my guitar. I looked at him, confused, and wanted to walk to him for clarification. I looked at Mark as Josh and Damien nodded to me, indicating they were ready, and it was time to start.

"Good evening, and welcome to the Midnight Cove," I announced into my microphone. I looked at Mark and smiled." We are Love

Stick." God, I hated that fucking name more every time I had to say it. "Enjoy the show."

Josh sat up straight on his drum throne, clicking his sticks. "One, two... One, two, three, four." The cymbals crashed in my ears, and the evening had begun. Nothing but the music mattered now, and we played like a well-rehearsed machine, always pretending this was the first time we played these songs.

The truth was, I was thirty years old, and I had played these songs a thousand times. This was going to be my last shot at doing something with music, and I had no other skills. Mark was the reason we had the shot. Well, that and my awesome guitar playing.

His voice pulled in the ladies, but my guitar finesse pulled in the boys and the musicians. Josh and Damien kept us in sync, and I felt that as a band, we were developing the synergy that only time could create.

I was happy to be on this tour so I could keep an eye on Mark while giving him the live experience he needed. I knew being in front of an audience was the best way to improve and become a seasoned player, but I also knew the pitfalls of playing in the clubs.

The gnawing reality that writing our own material was the only way to escape this trap weighed heavily on my mind. One hit song would take us to the top, and I could throw up kneeling on a clean marble floor instead of in these piss and shit-smelling stalls. Without a hit, we would bang it out in these rusty buckets of regret for the rest of our lives.

I decided then and there. It was time to introduce some of our originals into the show. When we returned to LA, we would have a band meeting to discuss returning to our day jobs and concentrating on writing originals. We had to make it, and this band was the best shot any of us would get.

I spotted my fantasy for the night, watching us from the dance floor, smiling. The night was looking up, and I felt good about life for the first time in years.

The Beginning

Some people are destined for greatness. Some are born into power and privilege. Some are thrust into success. Others fight their way to the top, stopping at nothing to achieve their goals.

Most of us, however, will settle for mediocrity. We will become ordinary and doomed to the darkness and invisibility failure brings as it continuously bites at the heels of our thoughts, actions, words, dreams, and inequities.

I'm not sure how one person can turn out so differently from others. I mean, we're all born with the same things...well, most of us. We all start naked and cold. Most have the love of a family. Others have no one and struggle to meet their basic needs.

Unfortunately, too many of the rich and powerful rely solely on their fortune and birthright of privilege. In the end, many of them seem to achieve the same ordinary life of mediocrity as the rest of us.

Many do nothing with their lives, living off the family name and fortune, never knowing what it's like to feel the joy of success or the sting of failure.

Most of us will start the fight to get to the top, but no matter how hard we fight. No matter how hard we try. We just can't seem to live up to our dreams. We will inevitably destroy the people we love in the process.

There are, however, things we all share. Whether rich or poor, the lure of drugs, alcohol, and sex are there for the taking. We all have an innate desire to self-medicate.

To use substances to calm ourselves and make us forget about the pain of the day, the week, the years, or the decades of our lives. The only difference between the rich and the poor regarding life's vices is the purity, the quantity, and, of course, the cost.

While the poor and ordinary experiment with drugs that can be fatal, the rich and extraordinary have the advantage of the best chemists and the best materials available.

The effects are the same, but the side effects and outcomes can be very different. The consequences are always more dire for the destitute and less fortunate.

The risk of being ordinary isn't just for the poor, however, and just as the rich can fall into the ordinary, the ordinary can reach for extraordinary and become elite.

On January 8th, 1935, Elvis Presley was born in Tupelo, Mississippi. On August 18th, 1938, Robert Johnson became the first member of the Twenty-Seven Club. During that time, black blues musicians paving the way for white rock n' roll musicians of the future were thought of so lowly that there wasn't even an autopsy or a cause of death on their death certificates.

Robert Johnson would be remembered as the guitarist who sold his soul to the devil. He would have movies written about him, and he would sell millions of albums even though he only recorded twenty-nine songs.

The man who posthumously won a Grammy and significantly influenced rock and blues artists worldwide would die poor, frightened, and alone.

At age eighteen, Elvis Presley walked into Memphis Recording Service to record two songs for his mother's birthday. Sam Phillips, who ran the Memphis Recording Service and would create Sun Records, saw Elvis's uniqueness and signed him to a recording contract.

Elvis released his first song, "That's Alright," when he was nineteen. At twenty-one, he had recorded three albums, providing the world with alternate renditions of "Blue Suede Shoes," "Heartbreak Hotel," "Hound Dog," and many more. His legacy had begun. He would soon become the best-selling artist of all time, and the world would crown him the king of rock n' roll.

He brought black rhythm and blues to white audiences, and they paid him handsomely for doing so. From his beautiful baritone range to his crazy legs and rotating hips, everything he did was a hit with the kids of the time. The rebel, a bad boy, had been born, and no matter how much the adults of the time wanted, there was no way to stop the cultural revolution that was beginning to take shape.

The government could make Ed Sullivan only show Elvis from the waist up because of his rotating hips. They could make him join the army and disappear for a few years because of their fear of his influence. But they couldn't stop what he represented, and most of all, they could never silence the music he influenced.

It's thought that Elvis stole the songs he recorded from the artists who wrote them. The truth could be considered even more sinister. Colonel Tom Parker negotiated his first contract, stating that Elvis would receive one-third of the writing credit for recording the songs. He would also receive a fifty-fifty split of the publisher's share.

By 1957, Elvis also received a one-third cut of mechanical royalties. Most of the artists who paid the price of allowing him to sing their songs thought that owning part of a number-one hit was much better than owning all of a song that no one would ever hear. They gladly signed on.

Twenty-seven years later, I was born on the same day as Elvis. It was January 8th, 1962. Elvis was burning up the charts with "Can't Help Falling in Love," and John F. Kennedy was dealing with the Cuban Missile Crisis.

Chubby Checker was making history on the airwaves with his song "The Twist," and the Tokens' famous tune "The Lion Sleeps Tonight" was roaring up the charts. My parents were young and still madly in love. God answered their prayers for a happy family with my birth, and we became the perfect illusion of one.

It's good we're born oblivious, as their constant fighting began soon after. When they weren't fighting, they were drinking and having friends over to partake in their excess. The addition of more people would lead to accusations and increased fighting.

It was a vicious pattern, and their dreams of a happy family were quickly becoming a distant memory. I was left to scrounge for myself or handed to anyone who would take me and show me some attention. Usually, they carted me off to bed so I was out of the way.

My earliest memory is of a man standing in our doorway with blood streaming down his forehead. The blood was being diverted to one side of his face by his crooked nose. I couldn't have been more than two or three years old. To this day, I'm not sure what happened, but it was etched in my mind forever. The rest of my memories weren't much better.

In 1961, John F. Kennedy succeeded Dwight D. Eisenhower as President of the United States. On November 22nd, 1963, Lee Harvey Oswald assassinated John F. Kennedy in Dallas, Texas.

The British Invasion officially began in 1964 with the Beatles' arrival in the United States. It marked a significant shift in music history. Four months later, the Rolling Stones followed, with a vision of reintroducing American audiences to the blues. They would eventually become the greatest rock band of all time.

The Vietnam War had been simmering for years, and in 1965, young people were burning their draft cards during protests against the war.

Also in 1965, an assassin's bullet killed Malcolm X, the man who spearheaded the Civil Rights Movement. Six months later, the Watts riots occurred in Los Angeles. Authorities reported thirty-four deaths, and rioters inflicted over forty million dollars in property damage during the six days of carnage.

By 1966, anti-Vietnam protests were sweeping America. Grace Slick and Jefferson Airplane released *Takes Off* and *Surrealist Pillows*, featuring the psychedelic song "White Rabbit," which many thought was called Go Ask Alice. John Lennon stated the Beatles were "more popular than Jesus." Five months later, they released the album *Revolver*.

Also, in 1966, Charles Whitman ascended the University of Texas clock tower carrying a trunk full of weapons. He would discharge ninety-six minutes of terror, killing fourteen and wounding thirty-one. This shooting would become the guide for mass shootings in America.

The Rolling Stones released their fourth studio album, *Aftermath*. The Beach Boys released *Pet Sounds*, and The Paul Butterfield Blues Band released their second album, *East-West*.

Frank Zappa and the Mothers of Invention released *Freak Out*. Jacqueline Susann published her book "Valley of the Dolls." John Mayall and Eric Clapton became the Bluesbreakers and released their self-titled debut. The Who released their debut album, *The Who Sings My Generation*, and the first color television transmission occurred in Canada.

America, it seemed, was going to hell in a handbasket, but the music industry was heating up. In 1967, Janis Joplin and her band,

Big Brother and the Holding Company, made their first appearance at the Monterey Pop Festival.

The Doors released their first album, and their hits "Light My Fire" and "Love Me Two Times" were playing on the radio. I caught my first groove dancing to those songs as they rumbled through our home and into my soul.

Future generations would remember 1967 as the summer of love, as the hippie movement overran Haight-Ashbury, filling the streets with peace and free love. Jimi Hendrix was doing his first concert in London. Jeff Beck was gaining prominence in the United States, and the Green Bay Packers defeated the Kansas City Chiefs in the first Super Bowl.

The Who released their second album, *Happy Jack*. Pink Floyd, with Syd Barrett on lead vocals, put out their first album, *The Piper at the Gates of Dawn*. It would reach number six on the UK album charts.

In 1967, I was five years old, and the counterculture was in full swing. Protest songs reflected the times, and acid metal reflected the drug culture of the day. Peace and free love permeated the minds of the young. But not all was happy and well.

It was also the year my father left. I would never see or hear from him again. After his departure, Mom tried to become the perfect mother by giving me the attention I so desperately craved. In between her depression, sobbing, and outbreaks, she would tend to my needs and somehow make me feel safe.

On April 4th, 1968, James Earl Ray assassinated Martin Luther King Jr. Two months later, on June 6th, Sirhan Sirhan assassinated John F. Kennedy's brother, Robert (Bobby) Kennedy. Pink Floyd, fired co-founder, lead singer, guitarist, and songwriter Syd Barrett, and Jethro Tull released their debut album, *This Was*.

Steppenwolf released their self-titled debut album. It would contribute to the growing counterculture by giving the rebellious anthem "Born to Be Wild" and the anti-drug song "The Pusher" commercial success. It also gave a new musical genre a name with the line "Heavy Metal Thunder."

1968 was also the year my mother came home with one of her Knights in white shining armor boyfriends. I was cast to the side, as I had been so many times before, playing second fiddle to "The man who was going to make everything okay."

In the beginning, as long as alcohol and drugs flowed freely, they seemed to get along well, and everything went smoothly. Mom appeared to be happy and content.

When the alcohol dried up and the drugs were gone, things would get tense, and he would slap us around. Fighting seemed to become a theme in our home, and I would sit in horror, watching the violence while listening to the yelling and screaming that accompanied it.

When he left a year later, my mother was six months pregnant, and the depression, crying, and fits of rage became uncontrollable. I think I was around six or seven years old at this time and had no idea what to do. I quickly became the comforter and parented her through her difficult times. This would remain our pattern for years to come, and it seemed I was destined to have an ordinary life devoid of all meaning.

On August 15th-18th, 1969, the world witnessed three days of peace and love when thirty-two popular bands of the day and five-hundred-thousand people descended on Woodstock, New

York. This was undoubtedly the most phenomenal concert in history and one of the most tremendous victories the hippie movement ever achieved. Peace and love had found their place among humankind. Or so it seemed.

Santana's self-titled debut album hit the record store shelves four days after their drummer, Michael Shrieve, stole the show at Woodstock, raising the bar for drummers everywhere. At the same time, Tommy Bolin began making a name for himself in Boulder, Colorado, with his band Zephyr.

Also in 1969, officials in New Jersey confiscated thirty thousand albums aptly named *Two Virgins* by John Lennon and Yoko Ono for violating pornography laws. Tommy James and the Shondells released "Crimson and Clover," *and* Michael Jackson made his first show appearance on The Ed Sullivan Show with his four brothers. They simply called themselves The Jackson 5.

Creedence Clearwater Revival released three albums in 1969, including *Bayou Country, Green River,* and *Willy and the Poor Boys.* Southern rock originated with the Allman Brothers' release of their self-titled debut album. The New York Jets upset the Baltimore Colts in Super Bowl II, and Brian Jones joined the Twenty-Seven Club after being fired from the Rolling Stones during the *Let It Bleed* Album. It would be released four months after his death.

Led Zeppelin released their second album. The Who released *Tommy*, and Neil Diamond released *Brother Love's Traveling Salvation Show*. Neil Armstrong became the first man to walk on the moon, and David Bowie released "Space Oddity" nine days earlier to coincide with the historic event.

Elvis Presley released "Suspicious Minds." The Band released their self-titled album, and the Motion Picture Association released the movie *Midnight Cowboy* with an X rating.

The film *Easy Rider*, starring Peter Fonda and Dennis Hopper, premiered in movie theaters, resonating deeply with the counterculture movement. It was the first movie to use pre-recorded songs instead of an original score. The soundtrack album catapulted songs like "Born to Be Wild," "If 6 Was 9," and "The Weight" into cult-like status. They quickly became synonymous with the hippie movement and counterculture of the day.

On December 6th, 1969, The Grateful Dead staged a free concert in Altamont, California, dubbing it the "Woodstock of the West." They had scheduled six bands, including the Rolling Stones, to play.

The Rolling Stones decided that hiring the Hells Angels as bouncers was a good idea. They then agreed that paying them Five-hundred dollars in beer would be the best payment choice for their services.

When the Stones hit the stage, all hell broke loose, and one of the Hells Angels stabbed a man to death as he approached the stage. The Grateful Dead never got to take the stage. The media of the day also reported three other accidental deaths, as well as many injuries and stolen cars.

After Woodstock's three days of peace and love energized the hippie movement and counterculture, the media of the day announced that the violence that occurred at Altamont signaled the end of the counterculture. The hippies and Haight Ashbury would fade, and hate and violence would replace peace and love once again.

Although Altamont was seen as the official end of the 1960s, its music still infused the culture and airwaves. The drugs created during this era would remain and continue to drench American culture. The 1960s never really ended. They just evolved.

The drugs became more prominent, and the blues-based acid rock of the 1960s gave birth to heavier branches on the musical family tree. Those branches sprouted more branches, and the protest songs that enveloped peace, love, and drugs turned into the songs we hear today. Like most things in our society, it wasn't necessarily for the best.

Mark

On December 25th, 1969, my little brother Mark was born. There would be no Christmas tree or Christmas lights that year, and Santa would not make his yearly appearance for me.

I slept in a hospital waiting room, wondering if this was going to be the time my mother would abandon me entirely, and I would have to face the world alone.

In the nurse's defense, they tried to sit with me and make me feel better by singing Christmas carols, but in the end, my greatest fears would come to pass.

I want to tell you I embraced Mark, fell in love, and immediately felt the bond of brotherhood... But the truth is that we were almost eight years apart, and when it came time to bring him home, I was confused and feeling a twinge of jealousy.

I thought it was something all older siblings felt on the first day of welcoming a new sibling into their lives, but something felt wrong. It was as if I had lived this scene before.

I wish I could say that the bond developed as the years went by, and we became close like brothers should. But we didn't. In fact, the older he became, the weirder I thought he was, and the more impending doom I felt.

I used to imagine we were the reincarnation of two soldiers in the Vietnam War, and that I was the reason for his death. Now, as my penance, I was responsible for righting my wrong, and I wanted nothing to do with it. Weird, I know, but such are the thoughts of children.

My mother was working at a utility company, keeping books or some shit like that, before Mark was born. Even with all the missed work when Mark's father left, they gave her two weeks of paid time off, which she used for maternity leave.

When she came home, the adrenaline rush of having a new baby in the house and the urgency of knowing she would be back to work put her into supermom mode. She spent her time cooing over Mark and ensuring his needs were met.

She swore more than once that she was done with alcohol and drugs and promised we would have a better life. I didn't mind the nonsensical talk or being permanently second in line. I didn't mind the mood swings or depression. I even accepted the orders: "Go get a diaper, go get wipes. Boil some water, etc."

With all the attention bestowed upon Mark, I could wander the neighborhood and find other things to occupy my time. His incessant crying only awakened me periodically, and I was becoming comfortable with my new situation and newfound freedom.

After two weeks, Mom returned to work, and I returned to school. The constant temptation from her friends crushed her defenses, and the party started again.

Her adrenaline rush crashed back into depression, and I found myself up at two or three in the morning, trying to get her to wake up and take care of Mark. His crying was affecting my sleep and driving me crazy. She never woke up to help.

I had no choice but to become Mark's parent, sitting in a rocking chair and feeding him with a bottle. My resentment of him grew, and I wished something terrible would happen, eliminating him from my life. As soon as he fell asleep, Mom would wake up and scream that I needed to get Mark ready for school.

On April 10, 1970, Paul McCartney announced the Beatles were disbanding. On September 18th, 1970, Jimi Hendrix joined the Twenty-Seven Club, dying in London, England. Janis Joplin would join him on October 4th, 1970. The day of the acid rock and flower power movement was coming to an abrupt end.

While 1970 was bidding farewell to the 1960s, a new era began when three guys from Flint, Michigan, took to the road from 1969 to 1971. They released the first live Grand Funk Railroad album, *Mark, Don, and Mel,* in 1972.

The raw power, distortion, and fast-driving rhythms would breathe new life into music. A new branch of the rock n' roll tree began to sprout, even though it would take years for the driving rhythms to take hold in the American psyche.

1971 continued the main branch of rock, growing more extensive and at an accelerated rate, as April Wine and REO Speedwagon released their self-titled debut albums. Even Led Zeppelin seemed to take a different direction in 1971 with the release of their best-selling album, *Led Zeppelin IV*.

Jethro Tull released *Aqualung,* The Who released *Who's Next*, and pioneers of heavy metal, like Alice Cooper, Mountain, Black Sabbath, Judas Priest, and Blue Öyster Cult, were all making their way into the spotlight.

The 1960s continued its slow demise in 1971 with the release of The Doors' last album, *LA Woman*. Jim Morrison joined the Twenty-Seven Club when he died three months later on July 3rd, 1971. Duane Allman followed when, on October 29th, 1971 he was traveling at a high rate of speed on his Harley-Davidson motorcycle.

With the release of the album *Eat a Peach* in 1972, the story on the street was that he crashed into a peach truck. The truth was even more horrifying. He ran into a flatbed boom truck that had stopped abruptly in front of him.

The motorcycle landed on top of him, crushing his internal organs. He was twenty-four and one of the greatest players of his time, writing the intro to "Layla" for Eric Clapton and creating his own version of American Southern Rock.

1972 was a surprising political year. Several government entities began to investigate the Watergate scandal as the American people elected Richard Nixon, the thirty-seventh President of the United States of America.

The counterculture tried desperately to hold on to its 1960s roots as The Doobie Brothers released *Toulouse Street*, Wishbone Ash released *Argus*, Chicago released *Chicago V*, and The Nitty Gritty Dirt Band released *Will the Circle Be Unbroken*.

Technology took hold when Atari introduced the first commercially successful video game, *Pong*. Alice Cooper found commercial success with *School's Out*. Jethro Tull released their concept album *Thick as a Brick,* and Blue Öyster Cult released their self-titled debut album.

Deep Purple released the metal masterpiece *Machine Head*, and Neil Diamond released his live album *Hot August Night*. The movie *Superfly* was released, and Curtis Mayfield's soundtrack permeated our beings and ears.

Eight members of the Palestinian militant organization Black September infiltrated the Olympic Village in Munich, West Germany, killing nine members of the Israeli Olympic team.

Mott the Hoople released *All the Young Dudes*. Jackson Browne released his self-titled debut album. Steely Dan released Can't *Buy a Thrill*. David Bowie released *The Rise and Fall of Ziggy Stardust and the Spiders from Mars,* and the Rolling Stones released one of the best rock albums ever made with *Exile on Main Street*.

In 1973, Elton John emerged into the spotlight with *the release of Goodbye Yellow Brick Road*. Tommy Bolin joined the James Gang. Led Zeppelin released *Houses of the Holy*, and the United States ended its direct involvement in the Vietnam War.

The Doobie Brothers released *"Long Train Runnin'."* Alice Cooper released *Billion Dollar Babies*. Pink Floyd released *Dark Side of the Moon,* and Aerosmith released their self-titled debut.

Steely Dan was distinguishing itself as one of the best underrated bands of all time with *Do It Again,* and Grand Funk Railroad was going commercial with the release of We're *an American Band.*

Southern rock was making its mark when The Allman Brothers, without Duane, released "Ramblin' *Man*." Deep Purple's "Smoke on the Water" and Edgar Winter's classic "Frankenstein" kept the heavy rock of the day alive.

REO Speedwagon was releasing their smash hit "Riding the Storm Out," Blue Öyster Cult was giving us *Tyranny and Mutation,* and The Who gave us *Quadrophenia*. It was also the year I started junior high school.

Things calmed down in our home as Mom found a new knight in shining armor named Ken. Even though they still liked to party, they both had steady jobs, and Mark was in a daycare center until they picked him up after work.

They seemed to genuinely like each other and were happy. This gave me time with my friends, and I began the party lifestyle my upbringing had taught me since I was born.

I attended my first school dance that year, and the world changed for Mark and me. David Essex's song "Rock On" was playing in the gym. If you've never heard that song, seriously, find a copy and listen to it. The bass line got me moving and feeling things I had never felt before. When the vocals came in, I was forever hooked on music and curious about who James Dean was.

Ken was pretty cool, and I hoped he would stick around for a while. He was a little younger than Mom and seemed to understand kids better because of it. He never yelled at us. And with his party lifestyle, he never had a problem with my friends coming by and hanging out. As long as we stayed downstairs, stayed out of his and Mom's way, and kept the madness to a minimum, they never even came down to check on us.

My friend Jim had a sister who was almost fifteen years older than he was, and she had a mind-altering album collection of artists from the 1960s and early 1970s. As we were looking through it, we found a small bag of marijuana in the jacket cover of Jimi Hendrix's *Are You Experienced* album.

It must have been there for years, as she never missed it. We smoked it while listening to the hallucinogenic sounds of Jimi Hendrix, Janis Joplin, Led Zeppelin, Joe Walsh, and the acid rock king himself, Jim Morrison.

She told me when I met her again later in life that, "One day, I just knew it was time to stop smoking weed." She knew the weed we found was still in the album jacket and that we smoked it. But in her words, it didn't matter because it was ragweed, and she wanted to get rid of it anyway. I always hoped I would get to that point, but it seemed I never would.

I remember it wasn't very potent, especially by today's standards, and the term ragweed became etched in my mind. Later that year, I would experience the actual effects of the plant.

Jim and I were young when we found his sister's stash. Eleven or twelve, and we thought we were the most grown-up people in the world puffing on that loosely rolled joint, coughing uncontrollably with each puff.

We listened to the songs, fantasizing that we were on stage playing them. Eventually, we got off the floor and played air guitar and sang air vocals.

Crosby, Stills, Nash, and Young released "Suite Judy Blue Eyes" in 1969. We heard it in 1973, and it became a staple of ours for our All-Star Air Band Jamboree. Jim's sister's record collection seemed endless. It had everything, and we returned every day listening to every album in her collection.

Getting stoned and listening to the Jimi Hendrix Experience was like an epiphany. I thought his guitar spoke directly to me. It was as if these rock stars understood the meaning of life and the secrets of the universe. I wanted to know them too. I knew right then, in my stoned little mind, that this was what I wanted to do for the rest of my life.

Soon after finding this mind-blowing music, I told my mother the only thing I wanted for my birthday, Christmas, or any other holiday for the rest of my life was a guitar.

It wasn't long after that when Mom came home early from work. It was so unexpected that I had to rush my friends outside and try to wave the cigarette smoke out after them.

Cigarettes were still cool at this stage of my life, and television commercials verified how cool they were. Smoking marijuana would soon become the most rebellious thing we could do, and we embraced it.

Mom came in with a smile, and Ken pulled into the driveway after her. They hardly seemed to notice the room full of smoke or the smell of tobacco in the air. Looking back, they had to have smelled our illicit extracurricular activities, but as I said, Ken was pretty cool, and he probably overlooked it. Mark opened his mouth as if to say something, but Mom was in a hurry and didn't seem to notice his nicotine-induced state.

"Come to my car with me," she smiled.

She rushed back to her car with me following and opened the trunk. Inside was the largest guitar I'd ever seen. I excitedly returned to the house, guitar in hand, and sat on the couch.

I couldn't even wrap my arm around the top of it to strum the strings. Using my fingers to push against the strings was not the experience I had imagined, and I wondered how anyone could play something like this.

She was so happy she could get it for me, and the smile on her face is what I remember most...well, apart from the monstrosity of the guitar. Later, I found out she was at a garage sale. When she saw the guitar, she called Ken, and he dropped everything to meet her there to check it out. I think it was five bucks, and well... the price was right for them.

Soon after that, she set me up with guitar lessons. It was in an old 1960s hippie's house, and when she opened the door, you could smell the wisps of herbs in the air.

A vision of her waving burning sage sticks as she walked through the rooms, exorcising evil spirits, came to my mind. *Maybe she worried I was going to be an evil spirit,* I thought as we sat on her couch. She giggled as she saw me pull the giant guitar out of the case and place it on my knee.

She tried to teach me Simon and Garfunkel's "69th Street Bridge Song" or some shit like that and commented that maybe the guitar wasn't the right one for me to start with.

The look on my mother's face when that lady told her I needed a smaller guitar to start with was enough to stop me from playing. I never returned for another lesson, and I don't remember trying to play that guitar again.

Mark seemed to enjoy grabbing the strings, pulling them, and listening to the loud b-o-o-i-i-n-g-g-g-g-g sound they made as they hit the metal frets below, so I kept it downstairs where we hung out.

One day, when my friends were over, I picked it up and gave my best Jimi Hendrix imitation, smashing it on the floor. If I had a can of lighter fluid and a lighter, I would have lit it on fire, too.

I don't know if you've ever tried to smash an acoustic guitar like that, but they're made really well. Smashing it takes a lot of effort and more than one smash on the ground. I bet I swung and hit the floor with it for fifteen minutes before the neck detached from the body, hanging on by the strings.

I continued to swing it repeatedly, eventually stomping on it to finish the deed. I sat on the couch, breathing hard, my arms feeling like rubber. I looked at the stunned faces of my friends, and laughter soon filled the air.

I didn't care. I had other things on my mind. My body was changing, and girls were consuming my thoughts. My days were busy, meeting one of my female classmates in the announcer's booth at the local rodeo grounds or pitching a tent in my backyard so I could invite the next-door neighbor in.

Making out was the greatest thing my brief life had experienced, and I couldn't get enough. Sex was never part of making out. Just heavy kissing and maybe a feel of second base if the rock gods smiled down on me.

The adrenaline rush of that first kiss and the first time touching a girl's breast was intoxicating. When I got older and advanced to dating, I would get a thrill thinking I was touching my date's breast as my arm was around her. When the lights came up, I would find that it was her elbow or some other inconsequential part of her body. I would lose my erection, but the fantasy would stay in my mind.

Phalanx

In 1974, "Freebird" and "Sweet Home Alabama" were blasting on FM radio stations. President Richard Nixon resigned from office, proclaiming he was "not a crook." "Killer Queen" from Queen and "Rikki Don't Lose That Number" from Steely Dan were climbing the charts.

The humorous "Spiders and Snakes" and "Wildwood Weed" by Jim Stafford made their way into the top 40. The Stones hit it hard with *It's* Only Rock' N' Roll," and David Bowie sang "Rebel, Rebel."

It was also the year Aerosmith released their second album, *Get Your Wings,* with the classic hits "Lord of the Thighs," "Woman of the World," and "Mama Kin." Blue Öyster Cult followed their classic album *Tyranny and Mutation* with *Secret Treaties*. Bad Company released their self-titled debut, and Michael Schenker's UFO was making its way on the scene. The music was transforming, and the heavy, angry riffs of the day were shaping a new generation.

During the summer of 1974, I was twelve and Mark was four. I had finished my first year of junior high school and was preparing for seventh grade. Mark was getting ready to start kindergarten, and my mother was obsessed with the cute clothes she was buying him for the occasion. It was also the year I met someone who would become my best friend, and I would get three friends in one.

Sometimes, the universe delivers events so strange that they defy even the imagination. Fate almost smiles down during these times, and today, fate smiled at me.

I was about to meet three friends who would introduce me to a world I was still years away from experiencing. They were all named Mike. They were all older than me, each a year older than the previous, and they all loved to party. We called them the three Mikeateers.

I met the first Mike when he almost ran me over with a motorcycle. We were both riding in a large vacant lot, which we turned into a mock motocross track. I was riding a bicycle, and Mike started riding his motorcycle on the same trail I was on. But for some reason, he was going in the opposite direction and headed straight for me.

I turned my tire trying to avoid a collision, and my bicycle and I got rocketed into a barbed wire fence. Mike panicked, dropped his motorcycle, and galloped to where I lay. I smiled as he looked down

50

at me, offering his hand. We instantly became best friends, and the next day, he introduced me to the other two Mikes in a ditch next to the school.

The other Mikes and I bonded instantly. Our ages were markedly different, but we wouldn't be apart until after they graduated from high school. The new Mikes were old enough to drive, but neither could afford a car, so sitting in that ditch getting high before school was a morning ritual of theirs.

It was the first time I smoked marijuana that had an effect on me, and I laughed so hard I thought I was going to die. When the school bell rang, a sense of paranoia set in. As I walked into school, I could feel everyone staring at me. I was positive they knew I was high.

The second bell of the morning rang, signaling that class was about to begin. I walked through the door to my first class of the day, and everyone's eyes, including the teacher's, watched as I walked down the row of desks before mine to avoid the teacher's glare.

This was an unfamiliar path, and I misjudged the angled wall at the back. With a thud, I walked into the wall with full force. My books and pencils dropped to the ground as I let out a painful grunt.

A roar of laughter rang through the room. My face turned red, and my shoulder throbbed. I wondered if I had broken my shoulder as I grabbed my belongings with one arm and crawled to my desk.

They know. They have to know. I thought as I slithered into the chair. I put my arms on the desk, placed my head on them, and nodded off to sleep.

Getting high and going to school got easier as I built up a tolerance to the weed, and it wasn't long before smoking all day and experimenting with other drugs became my norm.

In 1975, Steely Dan played on jukeboxes while the Doobie Brothers and Bachman-Turner Overdrive were on the airwaves. The Vietnam War ended, Saturday Night Live debuted, and Bill Gates and Paul Allen created Microsoft.

Nazareth released their sixth studio album and hit commercial success with "Love Hurts." Aerosmith was getting ready to release its fourth album. Ted Nugent was hitting his stride with his self-titled album, marking the beginning of his string of hit records. Yes, was playing in the round, and Rush's first three albums were being worn out on our record and 8-track tape players.

Led Zeppelin's *Physical Graffiti* dominated the charts, while Pink Floyd was proving their writing prowess with *Wish You Were Here*. Tommy Bolin released his first solo album, *Teaser*, and then joined Deep Purple.

Evel Knievel made his record-breaking jump over fourteen buses at Ohio's Kings Island Amusement Park. Grand Funk Railroad released *Some Kind of Wonderful*, and Paul McCartney was flying high with Wings.

Jethro Tull was making its mark with "Bungle in the Jungle." Bad Company released their second album, *Straight Shooter*. Alice Cooper welcomed everyone to his nightmare, and Bachman-Turner Overdrive told everyone, "You Ain't Seen Nothing Yet."

Music was our life, and the music of the day became our soundtrack. The songs wrapped around me, each one feeling like it had been written just for us.

In 1975, I was at all the high school parties. We would smoke pot, do mushrooms, or take a hit of acid. In the mid to late 1970s, Red

Dragon and Green Dragon tabs of LSD were our preferred vehicle for hallucinatory tripping.

Chemists would take a small, thin piece of paper and measure eighth-inch by eighth-inch squares. They would stamp a dragon of the corresponding color onto each square and dip the paper in lysergic acid diethylamide.

The results were... well... mind-bending and life-changing. A bandmate told me years later that he stopped taking acid because it got him too close to God. After the trails stopped moving in your peripheral vision and the hallucinations stopped, being close to God was precisely what it felt like. Everything seemed so clear, and the world made sense.

We could figure out all the troubles in our lives as well as all the problems in the world. By the end of the trip, we would know how to solve all of them.

Well...until we finally got to sleep. By the time we woke up, we had forgotten everything. Carrying only memories of knowing we had the answers, losing them in the slumber of our dreams.

This feeling of knowing is why Timothy Leary famously said, "Turn on. Tune in. Drop out." He believed LSD was a shortcut to spirituality. A way to commune with God. A shortcut to opening the secrets of the universe. It's what the hippies were chasing during their counterculture movement in the 1960s. It's what we continued to chase during the 1970s.

At the end of the summer, a high school party was taking place. I was about to enter the eighth grade, and one of the Mikes wanted to try something special for this bash. He was meeting a friend who had Green Dragon Acid.

It would be our first time tripping, and our nervous adrenaline continued to build as we thought about it. Another Mike was going to his dealer to score a half ounce of weed, and the last Mike and I headed to the liquor store to buy cigarettes and look for someone to buy us beer.

Finding someone to buy beer was always easier than the drug deals. Drug deals never went easy. Either the dealer had disappeared for the night, or everyone was dry. Getting the drug you were looking for could take days. Tonight, we were in luck, and everything went according to plan.

The sun was setting as we all grouped back together in our favorite ditch next to the school. We decided to wait until we got to the party to drop the acid and passed around a pipe while drinking beer from the twelve-pack some college guy had purchased for us. He never gave us change, but at least he gave us the beer.

We arrived at the party around nine and placed the tabs of acid on our tongues. Cars were already parked on the street, and people were walking to the door. We walked into the house and followed everyone to the keg. We each poured a beer and headed back outside.

Drinking beer on acid is a lot like drinking beer on cocaine or speed. It never seems to do anything until you've had way too much, and then it just kicks your ass.

I was a little kid when I started attending these big high school parties. I was twelve when I attended my first one and found it strange how everyone accepted me. No one ever said anything when I got a beer or when I was tripping and stoned out of my mind.

I always thought it was because I looked older until one night, we were at the house of a classmate who was a year older than me. He had an older brother, and his mom and dad had just divorced.

I was sitting on the couch with a new friend of mine named Frank. My friend's mom was dancing, and I was high as hell. I heard Frank ask the mom if she had ever danced with the boy she was dancing with before. She acted like she didn't hear him, so I innocently asked the question again.

Pandemonium ensued, and the next thing I knew, I was standing outside with a twenty-something-year-old pushing me to the ground, kicking me, and telling me he was going to beat my ass. No one did anything. No one tried to help.

I was crying when he kicked me one more time, turned, and walked back to the house. Everyone was crowding the windows to see what was happening, and I could feel their eyes upon me. I was so embarrassed that I walked five miles home, sniveling and wiping tears from my eyes the entire way.

I often wondered if he was proud of himself for beating up a little kid. But that happened almost two years ago, and my fantasizing about killing him in the most horrendous of ways wasn't doing my buzz any good.

The LSD took a firm hold of my senses, and I started to peak. Drums and bass resonated through the walls, permeating the space where we stood. My thoughts turned from fantasies of torturing the man who had beaten me to the sounds now possessing my soul.

My first thought was someone had turned up the stereo, but damn, what a stereo it had to be. A guitar joined in, and I looked at

Mike, seeing through him. I turned almost zombie-like and walked towards the band playing in the next room.

Two guitar players, a bass player, and a drummer were instrumentally playing songs of the day. Their version of "Mama Kin" from Aerosmith made my heart beat irregularly as the bass line reverberated through my body.

I had never seen or heard anything like this. The girls went wild, and I could see the lust in their eyes as they tried to get the attention of the boys in the band. My head raced as I was visually and auditorily assaulted.

I thought back on the days of listening to Jim's sister's albums and of the giant guitar I had smashed. At that moment, I had an epiphany that this was what I would do with the rest of my life.

The intensity of the acid continued taking full effect as my mind tried to figure out the sensory overload it was being given. I stared at a banner someone had made out of a sheet that featured three mushrooms and the word "Phalanx."

The mushrooms on the sheet started to breathe as the music played. The band blurred into the trails they left behind, and I could see visions of the promised land while standing inside my world.

After that night, I associated the word phalanx with mushrooms. I imagined a magical strain of mushroom that would elevate you higher and take you further on your path of understanding. I must admit that it dismayed and saddened me when I later discovered that it referred to a military formation used by the Greeks in ancient times.

One of the Mikes caught my attention and brought me back to reality. He signaled for me to follow him outside, and I followed. We walked through the driveway, lighting our cigarettes. He stuck his finger down his throat, spewing beer and foam onto the ground.

He took a hit off his cigarette and looked at me. "Damn, I feel better," he smiled. "Let's go drink some more beer." I stood there smoking my cigarette and watching in amazement as he walked back to the house.

My mind was racing, and my thoughts were clear. Watching Mike puke his guts out and then act nonchalant about it was really disgusting, but something magical was happening inside me. Even though my endeavor of playing a musical instrument had only lasted one lesson, I could almost tell the notes they were playing.

I could see the next lead the guitar player ripped into. I walked inside just in time to see one of the guitarists sit behind an empty drum kit. He and the main drummer started a dueling drum solo. These were the most extraordinary people I had ever seen.

My mind started to go to work, and before I knew it, I had not only laid out a plan of how I could get money to buy a guitar, I had also laid out a step-by-step plan to become more extraordinary than the band I was watching. My mind was working overtime, and the direction I was to follow seemed not only achievable but easy. I would become the rock star I was destined to become.

The following day, I felt melancholy due to a lack of sleep and because I had forgotten the brilliant money-making and how-to-become-a-rock-star scheme from the night before.

As the brain fog cleared, I could clearly see the events from the previous night, but I struggled to remember even a sliver of my plan. I needed to figure out a way to make money and buy a guitar. I wanted the girls yelling my name. I wanted to be extraordinary, and I needed all the special perks that came with it.

The Mikes stopped by and fired up a doobie as I was explaining my dilemma. Mom yelled for me to go mow the lawn from upstairs. "The grass is getting deep, and the neighbors are complaining," she screamed.

Well, that's ridiculous, I thought. The grass is dead, and only weeds grow on our patch of dirt. *The damn busybody neighbors need to mind their own business and leave us alone.*

Mom yelled her command again. I looked at the Mikes, told them I'd catch up with them later, and headed outside to complete my chore.

I went to the garage and began rummaging through it. There were boxes, old bikes, and an old canoe. With all the shit packed in there, it could take all day just to find the damn lawnmower.

The old, rusted lawnmower appeared when I moved the first box. *Damn,* I thought, *it must be my lucky day.* I grabbed the gas can sitting next to it and shook it. It still had gas in it, so I filled the tank.

After mowing, listening to the rocks being thrown up from under the lawnmower, and feeling them hit my shins, I started to catch the rhythm of the work at hand. *This is my answer,* I thought. *I could mow lawns during the summer and make enough money to get a guitar.*

I formulated a plan as I put the hot mower back in the garage. I wiped the blood from my legs and headed to my room, lying on my bed, celebrating my great idea and fantasizing about the beautiful guitar that would soon be in my possession.

Crowds of people were watching me on stage. A backstage party materialized. Beautiful, willing girls and, of course, the drugs we would consume filled my head for the rest of the day. The fantasies stimulated my libido, and I quickly found myself in the shower, relieving my pent-up stress from the day.

Dream On

I spent that summer fantasizing, mowing lawns, and taking long, hot showers. As long as I timed it right, I could get really high and get a lawn done before I lost my buzz and concentration.

Depending on rocks and other obstacles, I could kick out a regular-sized suburban lot in an hour, maybe an hour and a half. Then, it was time to roll another joint and move on to my next venture.

Everyone must have been satisfied with my work, as my phone started to ring with referrals. At ten dollars a pop, I thought I would be rich by the end of the summer.

The shiny new sunburst Gibson Les Paul I had seen on a poster in a record store and fantasized about would soon be in my hands. Rock stardom was sure to follow.

Reality never turns out the same way our fantasies do. We always think about the good things that will happen to us, and our vision is always ahead and never looking down.

We don't fantasize so we can recognize pitfalls, yet somehow, we always fall into them. No matter how well we formulate our plan, and no matter how many drugs we take during its formulation, something always happens that we justify as being "out of our control."

This time would be no different. The Mikes had been buying drugs and alcohol for me for a long time. So, when word got out I was making money, they all looked to me to give back in kind.

The good news was that a lid of marijuana only cost ten dollars. Dealers never weighed the drug. Instead, they measured it with their fingers. It depended on the size of the person's fingers you were buying from as to how much you would receive.

Our favorite dealer was a high school heavyweight, state champion wrestler. His fingers looked like the cat tails growing on the side of our town pond. I swear he had the biggest, fattest fingers I'd ever seen. Sometimes, it seemed like we received an ounce and a half of weed for ten bucks.

During the seventies, marijuana was coming from Mexico. The Mexican government, with the aid of funding and helicopters from the United States, started spraying crops with paraquat, poisoning the buds. A higher grade, higher potency, and more expensive

Colombian sinsemilla was almost on our doorstep, and we were more than willing to partake.

Our dealer must have smoked some of the paraquat shit, as sometimes he would lose his mind and chase us around, shooting at us with a twenty-two caliber rifle. He was really fucked up in the head and thought it was funny to scare us.

He was the only pot dealer we could find that would sell to a bunch of kids. He never hit any of us, so he was either a terrible shot or not aiming. Still, his laugh and his screams were enough to make us shit our pants as we were running through the forest, looking for a place to hide.

When we ran out of weed a couple of weeks later, we would endure the horror again and return to his home for another bag. We would sit on his old, weathered couch, waiting for him to flip out.

It's unbelievable what a drug addict will endure when he's out of drugs and needs to score. And sure as shit, something would trigger him. We would find ourselves back in his nightmare, running for our lives with the crack, crack, crack of a twenty-two caliber rifle from behind us.

We smiled and giggled as we ran with a new bag of weed bulging in our front pants pocket, collapsing to the ground when we were far enough away. When we caught our breath, we would roll a joint and get high.

The city I lived in had a guitar/pawn shop called "Rocky Roller." A group of older 1960s hippies, who were musicians themselves, ran it. They were great guys and always very helpful, especially to us youngsters with stars in our eyes.

The Mikes weren't into the whole musical instrument thing, and when they were at work or busy, I would go to the local music stores to check out the new gear. I never played or even asked to hold one of the guitars.

I felt intimidated and would decline when the salesperson held one out, offering it for me to play. I was happy to just walk through the store, take in the eye candy, and add to my wish list the guitars I would buy when I became the greatest rock star of all time.

The first time I walked into "Rocky Roller," a beautiful white Gibson Les Paul Custom was hanging on the wall. It wasn't the 1959 cherry sunburst Les Paul that Joe Walsh sold to Jimmy Page in 1969, but it was love at first sight. At a price of six hundred dollars, it was what motivated me to work hard that summer.

Sixty lawns was my target, and I excruciatingly exceeded that number, earning almost seven hundred dollars. At the end of the summer, I pulled out the tin box where I stashed my money, unlocked the small lock securing it, and opened the top.

I pulled out the bills and counted. One hundred and fifty dollars was all I had left. I knew the guys at the guitar store would negotiate on the guitar, but one hundred fifty dollars?

The social life of a big shot fourteen-year-old supporting everyone's habits cost me most of my hard-earned money and the chance to follow my destiny. The term "A friend with weed is a friend indeed" had never rung truer. I took my hundred and fifty dollars to Rocky Roller, and they sold me an old Silvertone or some crap like that.

It looked like a weird, droopy Fender Stratocaster with knobs and switches on it. It had a primitive lever that, when pushed, allowed you to alter the note. The problem was that every time you touched it, it would go out of tune.

Hendrix had the same problem with his Stratocaster, but I'm sure it was mild compared to mine. It came with a small amp, so I really couldn't complain. I felt they had done me a favor. One hundred fifty dollars was cheap for a guitar, strap, amp, chord, and a handful of assorted picks.

Mom and Ken agreed to pay for a few lessons, so on my next visit to Rocky Roller, I asked if they knew any instructors. They pulled a phone number from a flyer hanging on a bulletin board behind them.

They knew this teacher personally and believed he was the best for beginners. When I called, he offered to come to my house, and we set a day and time for his arrival.

He was another old 1960s hippie with long blondish-brown hair and an old acoustic guitar in hand. I showed him my new Silvertone, and he didn't seem impressed.

He asked if he could have a glass of water and followed me into the kitchen. There was only Mark and me in the house, but being the naïve kid I was, I had no problems helping out the man who would help me on my way to stardom.

"You got anything to eat in that refrigerator?" He grinned

"I don't know. Help yourself," was my response.

I had opened the floodgates as he had a severe case of the munchies. He pulled everything out of the fridge that looked edible and spoke about music and other things over my head as he devoured everything in his sight. After he ate his fill, he belched and sat on the couch, pulling out his acoustic guitar.

He had written out the Beatles song. "Yellow Submarine" on a yellow legal pad. He looked it over and, pleased with his work, placed it in front of me. I couldn't get the fingering right, and it hurt when I pushed on the strings.

These old, broke, drugged-out musicians should have thrown up some red flags when I was choosing my future career. But when you're a kid, you're blinded by youth and don't think about obvious forewarnings like that.

When my mother showed up, shit hit the fan, and she stormed to the grocery store to buy something for dinner. She banned everyone from coming into the house when they weren't home and went so far as to never pay for another guitar lesson.

The new ban was actually a God-send for me. I might not have known how to make a G chord, but I knew I didn't want to learn this old 1960s acoustic crap. I was a rock star, and I wanted to learn rock songs.

I went back to Rocky Roller and explained what happened. They said I could hang out in the shop with them, and if they had time, they would show me some of the licks of the day.

They loved to jam when it was slow, and when customers came in, they were usually there to try out guitars, amps, or effects. Life was looking up, and I found myself there almost every day, helping with moving inventory and watching the everyday happenings of a music store.

They taught me the secret of the pounding rock of the day. POWER CHORDS. The easy-to-play two-note chords changed my world and allowed me to play easy rhythm hooks of the day like "Smoke on the Water."

It also allowed me enough playing time to build strength in my left hand. Making the proper fingerings for chords and scales was becoming more manageable.

I took everything the Rocky Roller guys said or showed me to heart. I learned everything I could from them. I took all the papers they gave me or that I had purchased and diligently practiced the chords and progressions on the pages.

They showed me basic guitar maintenance and helped me set up my guitar. They showed me how to change strings and how to lower the strings by shimming the neck or adjusting the bridge.

They taught me how to care for a rosewood fretboard and bring back its luster using lemon oil. But most importantly, they taught me about string gauges.

The strings that came with my guitar were an 11-52 gauge. They were hard to push on and impossible for me to bend. The Rocky Roller guys said that only cowboys and jazz players played with 11s. They introduced me to a thinner 9-46 gauge string that was easier to push on and bend.

Later, I found that playing an 8-42 gauge and replacing the high e with a 9-gauge high e helped to keep it in tune. I might have had a shit guitar, but after an hour in the store with them helping me set it up, it was playing easier. I was now ready to learn how to play the instrument I chose to make my life companion.

It didn't take long before I could make chord shapes and changes, albeit clumsily. Playing the song "Yellow Submarine" from The Beatles, which the old hippie had written out and left for me, became fun. I would strum the G chord and sing, "We all live in a...Change to the D chord and strum ...a Yellow submarine. A Yellow Submarine...

It took time to change from one chord to the next, but the Mikes seemed to like it, and Mark would dance around and laugh, enjoying his contact high. Everyone would sing along with me, stopping as I changed the chords and then chiming in again. Looking back, it was hilarious.

After learning these riffs and partial songs, it didn't take me long to form a band. Finding members was easy. I hung around outside the band room and waited until I heard someone jamming on the drums or the bass. Everyone wanted to be in a band, so when they came out of the room, I asked if they wanted to join the band I was putting together.

Jonathan was a drummer and was the first one to be recruited. He was taller and lankier than I was, and he wore thick black-rimmed glasses. His golden blond hair glistened in the sun, and I knew the chicks would dig him. A bass player proved to be more difficult.

Jonathan had a basement, and his parents were cool with us practicing there. I packed my stuff and asked one of the Mikes for a ride to his house. I set up my little amp, and we started playing. The little amp wasn't powerful enough, and I couldn't hear myself over his loud drums and cymbals. *More speakers*, I thought. *I need more speakers*.

During my lawn mowing career, when I was clearing out the garage, I stumbled upon a large wooden speaker cabinet with two twelve-inch woofers inside. I knew they would be perfect in my quest for more volume. After hooking them up to my stereo to ensure they worked, I went to bed, knowing that tomorrow I would be a better player.

The Mikes pulled up outside my house and honked. I grabbed my books, ran to the car, and jumped into the back seat. A joint was shoved in my face, and I hit it hard, holding the smoke in my lungs. Smoking weed had become my favorite sin, and smoking before going to school was a tradition we carried on for years.

The teachers didn't seem to mind the smell or that we would lie our heads on our desks, taking power naps during their class. At least they never said they did. Smoking weed became our normal, and staying straight was only for those who couldn't handle drugs.

Trying to maintain in school while tripping on acid was a different story. One wrong look, or a little giggle, triggered an unstoppable burst of full-fledged laughter.

A quick exit from the school grounds always seemed safest when that happened. The risk of getting called into the principal's office while tripping was inevitably a disaster. But it was a disaster that was too funny to resist.

Mom was pretty cool with me skipping school. I knew if I could get to her work and tell her I skipped before the school called her, she would back me up and tell them I had a doctor's appointment or make up some other lame excuse.

If I didn't let her know before they called, the call would surprise her, and they would suspend me for three days. She would yell at me for not informing her, and I would have a three-day vacation. Mom was the best. She tried to have my back, and I wondered if it was because of the horrible mother she was when I was a child.

After school, I packed my new speaker into the trunk of Mike's car, and we headed to Jonathan's basement for a jam. Jonathan was fearful of the drug scene. He was terrified that the smell of weed or cigarettes would reach his mom upstairs, so I would get "primed" beforehand.

I carried the big cabinet inside and set it next to my little amp. I placed the small amplifier, which contained one 10-inch woofer, on top of the tall wooden cabinet and plugged the large cabinet into it.

Then I plugged in my guitar, quickly ensured it was in tune, and Jonathan counted 1, 2, 3, 4. I ripped into a power chord, and the jam began.

I stumbled for a few seconds, almost shocked at being able to hear myself, and fell into the groove. The progression became effortless to play, and the chord changes were smooth and seamless.

I was in the pocket. That magical place where the music flows through you, not from you. I sounded good, and the new speakers were helping me become the player I knew they would. I moved to an A minor scale on the neck and played a short lead.

Suddenly, I breathed in a burning electronic smell. It's hard to describe that smell. I can only say that it smelled like burning wire hair. I turned around just as the sound from my guitar stopped, and black smoke wafted up from the back of my amp.

"Fuck," I yelled as Jonathan continued drumming until he saw the look on my face. Silence filled the room. I couldn't believe it. My amp, my trusty companion, was now a smoking wreck.

I wondered what caused it to go up in smoke like that. Whatever it was, it was too late to start worrying about it now, and I could see myself mowing lawns again during my summer break to get a new one.

I'm not sure how the universe works or why things work out, and I'm not sure I want to know, but the next day, two of my old customers called and left me messages letting me know it was time for their lawns to be mowed.

It wouldn't take long for me to rebuild my business, and with the money I earned, I would be back in the world of owning an amplifier and all the ear-splitting sound that would come through it.

Spontaneous Combustion

1976 was a pivotal year for rock and heavy metal. AC/DC released their album *Dirty Deeds Done Dirt Cheap* in Europe, Australia, and New Zealand, and E.M.I. signed the Sex Pistols to a recording contract. Jimmy Carter became the thirty-ninth President of the United States. The XXI Summer Olympic Games opened in Montreal, Canada, and the XII Winter Olympic Games opened in Innsbruck, Austria.

Judas Priest's album *Sad Wings of Destiny* defined them as a band, and Rush's *2112* album captured everyone's attention. Boston's first album changed guitar tones, and Tom Shultz's technical wizardry gave us the first headphone amplifier. Steve Jobs and Steve Wozniak started the Apple Computer Company. Tom Petty released his debut album, featuring the song "American Girl. A court found George Harrison guilty of subconsciously plagiarizing "He's So Fine" for his song "My Sweet Lord."

Heart released their debut album, *Dreamboat Annie*. Blue Öyster Cult broke into widespread fame with the song "Don't Fear the Reaper" on their *Agents of Fortune* album, and New York City's Son of Sam, in his first attack, killed one person and seriously wounded another.

Wild Cherry played that Funky Music. Nazareth lamented that "Love Hurts," Aerosmith was dreaming on, and Foghat was giving us "Slow Ride." Gregg Allman's testimony convicted Allman Brothers roadie Scooter Herring of providing drugs to the band. The judge sentenced Herring to seventy-five years in prison.

Kiss released their fifth album, *Destroyer*, launching them into rock god status. Queen Elizabeth II sent out the first royal email. Led Zeppelin released their first live album, *The Song Remains the Same*, and their seventh studio album, *Presence*.

Tommy Bolin released his second album, *Private Eyes*. He died three months later of a drug overdose during the promotional tour. He was twenty-five. Barbara Walters became the first female US nightly network news anchor, and Humble Pie's Peter Frampton released the biggest-selling live album in history with *Frampton Comes Alive*.

Thin Lizzy released their harmony two-guitar attack on "Jailbreak." Deep Purple disbanded. The Steve Miller Band was

Flying Like an Eagle, and Jethro Tull declared they were "Too Old to Rock and Roll but too Young to Die."

The movie *Rocky* was being released in movie theaters. Bob Marley's first album, *Rastaman Vibration*, introduced the world to reggae, and The Bee Gees' *Children of the World*, featuring "You Should Be Dancing," *marked* the beginning of the disco era. Music was changing, and this year was the catalyst for that change.

It was also the year I turned fourteen, was navigating my path of personal growth, and graduated from junior high school. High school would start in September, and the music landscape of 1976 was a catalyst for my evolution, influencing my friendships, aspirations, and understanding of the world.

Mark was turning seven in December, had made it through first grade, and would start second grade. Mom and Ken were settling into the family they had always wanted, complete with fighting, drama, and everything she had ever known. Our lives were changing with the times.

The Mikes were getting older. Two had graduated from high school, and one would graduate this year. They were so busy with work and being adults that I only saw them on weekends, and those were becoming less frequent.

People have a way of drifting apart, especially when the things they once had in common disappear. The Mikes were my first experience of losing friends because of this phenomenon. As much as I moved on, didn't dwell on it, and didn't show it, it hurt, and the abandonment I felt all my life again raised its ugly head.

Jonathan and I were improving. We could jam on standard blues progressions and get through some of the songs of the day. But the

73

chords were slow and sloppy. The strumming was irregular. The leads sucked. We still needed a bass player, and neither of us could sing. Other than that, we had an amazing band.

The parents of one of Jonathan's geek friends were going out of town, and he wanted to have a party that would make him the most popular kid in school. He planned on inviting the entire school and already had a keg lined up.

Jonathan told him about our band, and without hearing us, he asked if we wanted to play at his party. OUR FIRST GIG! We had so much to do. The thrill of our first performance was electrifying, and we were on cloud nine, ready to give it our all.

I was never popular with kids my age, but they thought I was cool because the Mikes were older than me, and I attended high school parties. My classmates couldn't experience what I did, either because they weren't allowed or because they didn't have the opportunity. Because of this, I thought they expected a lot from me, and I didn't want to disappoint them.

We started practicing every day to prepare for our debut. It didn't do much to improve us, but it distracted me from the butterflies flying in my stomach every time I thought about playing in front of people.

We spent most of our time getting stoned and thinking of a name. Initially, we threw around silly band names, including The Flying Pickles and The Phantom Zone, but ultimately settled on Spontaneous Combustion. As fate would have it, this name would prove to be both iconic and ironic.

We wrote a single-note riff and turned it into a song that alternated between blaring A and D power chords, which the hippies at Rocky Roller had shown me. Stardom was waiting for us, and we were ready and on time.

The aspen trees began to turn golden yellow, and summer gave way to fall. School would start the following week. The Mikes were always up for a party, so I called them and invited them to attend our gala premiere. Jonathan and I didn't have our driver's licenses yet, so I asked the youngest Mike if he would pick us up and haul our gear to the gig.

We loaded Mike's car with Jonathan's drums and my guitar amp. We crammed into the front seat, with me riding shotgun and holding my guitar between my legs. My heart pounded in my chest, and I felt motion sick as we wound down the dirt road toward our destiny.

We pulled into the driveway and quietly walked around back to check out where we would be playing. Mike lit a joint, and we sat on the ground looking at the valley, with patches of fall colored trees, below.

I fantasized about the applause, admiration, and girls we would receive after the gig. A sense of accomplishment washed over me and Jonathan as we set up. We had made it to our first gig, and we were ready to rock.

The house was two stories tall and had a walk-out basement. We set up under the wooden deck connected to the second floor and ran an extension cord through the sliding glass door behind us.

I plugged in my guitar with my wet, clammy hands, feeling like I wanted to vomit. My nerves were getting the best of me, but I knew I had to push through. This was our moment, and I was determined to make it a night everyone would remember.

We were discussing the best way to do a sound check when I saw the other Mikes pull into the driveway. I set down my guitar, and Jonathan, Mike, and I walked to their car, jumping into the back seat. We sat there smoking a joint and drinking a beer, taking the edge off my apprehension.

One of the Mikes handed me some psilocybin mushrooms. The stress I was experiencing was overwhelming, and self-medicating had worked before, so I tossed them into my mouth.

They tasted nasty and made me want to throw up even more. Instead of chewing, I swallowed and swigged a beer to eradicate the taste.

We drove off to get cigarettes, and a bottle of Wild Turkey 101 appeared during the ride. We started drinking from the bottle, and when we returned, the crowd was rolling in.

It looked like Jonathan's friend would accomplish his goal, as it seemed the entire school was showing up. Beer was going down easy, the mushrooms were kicking in, and the joints seemed to come at me nonstop.

Learning how to play an instrument is only part of the battle of being a rock star. Learning about acoustics and problems that could arise during a gig was another part of the equation. Unfortunately, you don't know what you don't know, and every new obstacle is a learning experience.

Playing outside without proper equipment is a bad idea. Getting more hammered than the audience is even worse. The old saying, "The drunker they get, the better we sound, but the drunker we get, the better we think we sound," is a painful but necessary lesson to learn.

My heart was beating so fast it felt like it would explode out of my chest. I could see my hands sweating, and my head became numb as the mushrooms took hold. Suddenly, it was showtime.

I stumbled to the stool my amp sat on and strapped on my guitar. Jonathan wobbled behind his drum kit. I looked at the people in the audience, and my heart beat even faster. Pain started to emanate in my chest, and I thought I was having a heart attack.

Jonathan clicked his sticks together and counted ... 1, 2, 3, 4 ... The alcohol and mushrooms exited my stomach and spewed onto the ground, splattering some of the front-row seekers as Jonathan's cymbals rang in my ears.

Everyone had a night they would never forget, and I had a night I couldn't remember. That night was something I never fully recovered from, both physically and mentally. I can't think of a time when I was more humiliated. The rock star comments haunted me as we entered high school, and I wanted to run away to the nearest crossroads to sell my soul to the devil just as Robert Johnson had done so long ago.

I justified the night in my mind by convincing myself that humiliation was part of the learning curve. *It was one of the best teachers,* I would think, while walking down the halls of my school.

It motivates you to improve, my inner voice would say as I walked past my peers, who were laughing as they mocked me with, "Can I have your autograph, rock star," or, "Oh my god, didn't you spontaneously combust?" I promised myself things would be different if I got in front of a crowd again.

Rock N' Roll High School

1977 was the year punk came into its own, adding girth to its branch of the musical tree. The Clash, the Ramones, Iggy Pop, and the Sex Pistols suddenly gained mainstream acceptance.

Also, in 1977, America received its first VHS-based video cassette recorder. Watching movies from home and recording your favorite TV shows to watch later became all the rage.

With the release of the movie and soundtrack to *Saturday Night Fever*, the Bee Gees developed a branch of the musical tree all their own. The slogan "Disco Sucks" became a common phrase as the rockers of the day expressed their distaste while secretly listening to the falsetto ensemble of the Gibb brothers, Barry, Robin, and Maurice. Imagine being so original that you created a music style, launching countless musicians who played your genre, producing number-one hits.

In 1977, Elvis Presley died at the age of forty-two. Studio 54 opened in New York. The release of the Atari Video Computer System revolutionized the video game industry. Police in Yonkers, New York, arrested postal worker David Berkowitz, accusing him of being the Son of Sam. Metal is still holding its own as our generation's preferred music, and Ted Nugent releases *Cat Scratch Fever*.

The first Apple II computer went on sale. AC/DC released *Let There Be Rock* in Australasia through the Albert Productions label. A modified international edition was released in the United States later in the year.

Kansas released *Point of Know Return*. Foreigner made their way onto the scene with their self-titled album, while Meat Loaf cemented his name in music history with *Bat Out of Hell*.

Days after Lynyrd Skynyrd released Street Survivors, southern rock suffered a blow. Their plane went down, killing three of the band members, including lead singer Ronnie Van Zant. The original album cover seemed to predict the horrible crash, with flames engulfing the band, and the record company quickly reissued the cover with the flames removed.

The first Star Wars movie opened in the cinemas. Steve Miller made his way up the charts with the songs "Jet Airliner" and "Jungle Love." Styx released *Grand Illusion* with the smash hit "Come Sail Away." It would become the theme song for our senior prom.

Judas Priest released *Sin After Sin.* Jethro Tull put out *Songs from the Wood.* Jimmy Carter raised the minimum wage from two dollars and thirty cents to three dollars and thirty-five cents an hour. Thin Lizzy released *Bad Reputation,* and Pink Floyd continued to release masterpieces with their new album, *Animals.*

Queen released *News of the World* with the Rock anthems "We Will Rock You" and "We Are The Champions." Eric Clapton earned his nickname with his album *Slowhand.*

The mini-series *Roots* premiered on ABC. Fleetwood Mac released their monumental album *Rumours,* and Blue Öyster Cult featured its biggest hit, "Godzilla," on its *Spectres* album.

It was also the beginning of my sophomore year of high school. Jonathan had gone by the wayside, and the Mikes had all but disappeared. They were busy working to support themselves and their habits and slowly faded away, finding new interests. I occasionally saw them at the local arcade, but they spent most of their nights at the bar on Main Street.

In January 1978, I turned sixteen and was halfway through my sophomore year of high school. Metal continued that year with the release of Black Sabbath's eighth album, *Never Say Die*, the last to feature Ozzy Osbourne. AC/DC, Ted Nugent, and Judas Priest also released new albums.

The first test-tube baby was born. The price of gold topped two hundred dollars an ounce, and Boston and Foreigner followed up their first albums. Thin Lizzy released *Live and Dangerous*. Steve Perry joined Journey, and Molly Hatchet released their self-titled debut album, proving that Southern Rock was still alive and well.

The Cars and Dire Straits released their first albums. The TV show *Dallas* premiered. Leon Spinks beat Muhammad Ali for the heavyweight boxing title, and Joe Walsh made his presence known again with his album *But Seriously Folks*.

Van Halen took the world by storm with their first album. Taito released the computer game *Space Invaders*. The Who released *Who Are You*. Blondie released Parallel Lines, which included "Heart of Glass," and authorities charged Sex Pistols guitarist Sid Vicious with the murder of his girlfriend, Nancy Spungen.

1978 was also the year I found my new best friend and drummer. Billy was a year younger than me, and his bass-playing classmate Tommy came with him. Tommy had a really cool fretless bass guitar that would whine as he played notes a little sharp or flat.

My playing was getting better, but I needed to improve faster. I never felt good enough, and that thought kept me in my bedroom, learning new licks every night after school. There weren't guitar teachers in our small town, and there weren't magazines or tablature.

I sat in front of my record player, trying to learn songs by lifting the needle and placing it back where I had just picked it up. I would repeat this over and over, trying to hear what they were doing while searching for the notes on my guitar. I scratched up and destroyed a lot of grooved vinyl, but it was the only way to learn.

Blue Öyster Cult was playing a show at Red Rocks Amphitheater in Denver on September 4th, 1978, and we decided to take the two-hour trip to see them. I think we paid eight dollars a ticket and had to fill up the gas tank at sixty-five cents a gallon. The three of us couldn't afford that cost alone, so we invited a fourth person to go.

Blue Öyster Cult had a stunning laser light show. I had seen them at McNichols Sports Arena the year prior, and it was psychedelic. When the lasers hit the mirrored balls, it literally rained laser beams. It was one of the most breathtaking things I'd ever seen, and I wanted to see it again in a different venue.

We arrived early and waited at the front of the line for the gates to open. We walked up the stone stairs looking for seats in the open-seating arena and couldn't help but notice a group of bikers sitting in the front row. The opening act blew Blue Öyster Cult away, and it was evident who the bikers were there to see.

That backup band was AC/DC. We had never heard of AC/DC and sat in awe as Bon Scott put Angus Young on his shoulders, running him up and down the wide stairs in the mile-high elevation. The high-octane raw rock n' roll they played was the envy of garage bands worldwide.

It wasn't long before the 8-track tape players in our cars were blasting the praises of this prodigious group. Hearing AC/DC for the first time and having a new drummer and bass player steered me further into my dreams of stardom.

Miraculous coincidences have happened throughout my life, repeatedly showing me that the career path I chose was the one I was destined to pursue. The fourth person who attended our road trip concert was a singer.

Maybe it was the drugs I would be doing over the next...well, the rest of my life, or perhaps it was that our acquaintance was for such a short time, but I really don't remember his name. So let's call him Stan. Stan was the man who quickly became part of my plan.

As we were driving to the show, we found out Stan could sing. He belted out the lyrics to songs we played on the car stereo, and his vocal range impressed us.

A few days earlier, our history class teacher had assigned a report. Since we were wanna-be rock stars, we presented our report as a skit with us playing a song with Stan singing.

Aerosmith had released their album *Rocks* in 1976, and Stan loved the song called "Sick as a Dog" featured on it. The lead work was reasonably short, and there was enough going on with chord and rhythmic changes that it was possible to delete the lead part and make a few adjustments to create the hack we needed to pull off an actual song.

Once again, it was time to find a name, and just like last time, we spent many stoned hours picking the perfect one. This was becoming one of the fun parts of being in a band.

We finally settled on The Growlers. We planned and well-rehearsed the performance. I started feeling the same butterflies in my stomach I felt before my and Jonathan's gig.

Only these weren't butterflies. They were larger. More like crows. I convinced myself they would subside. This was going to be the gig of my rebirth. A new beginning for my rock n' roll fantasy.

The report was our interpretation of "The History of Music," which began at the dawn of time. I was sweating and feeling unwell as Stan began the narrative of how humans first discovered two thick branches and a hollow log.

My stomach twisted, and I ran to the bathroom, emptying its contents. Billy began a four-count on his bass drum as I exited the bathroom. I ran to the stage and strapped on my guitar as he played his extended steady beat. My stomach settled, and I forgot about feeling sick as we played the song.

Our electric guitars echoed through the halls, leaving a lasting impression on the walls and the classrooms. The song wasn't a complete train wreck, and even though I wondered if I had a terminal illness, it felt like a win.

After class, I walked down the halls expecting the normal rock star comments, but they never came. For the first time, no one ridiculed me for wanting to be a music icon. The teacher gave us a C+ for originality and wrote a comment saying, "Why would anyone want to be sick as a dog?"

We never did another gig with Stan, and the band's name went with him. I'm not sure if he moved or if we drifted apart, but we soon returned to a three-piece ensemble jamming in my garage.

We had broken through the barrier of playing a complete song, and we were getting better. Our jams took on a confidence we hadn't experienced before, and playing songs by eliminating the leads or just jamming to chord progressions was coming together.

In 1979, during my junior year of high school, snow fell in the Sahara for the first time in recorded history. The release of *Highway to Hell* propelled AC/DC into a headlining act that filled concert halls. Tom Petty continued making his mark on music with *Damn the Torpedos*, proving his writing genius with "Don't Do Me Like That" and "Refugee."

The movies *Alien* and *Mad Max* debuted in movie theaters. Cheap Trick found their fame *Live at Budokan* and gave a quick follow-up with *Dream Police*. The Knack released one of the most successful debut albums of all time with *Get the Knack*, including the hits "My

Sharona" and "Good Girls Don't." The Clash released *London Calling*, and Sire Records released *Pretenders*, the debut album by Chrissy Hynde and The Pretenders.

Kiss tried its hand at disco with the album *Dynasty*, and movie star Ronald Reagan announced his candidacy for President of the United States. Van Halen followed up with their second album, *Van Halen II*, and Pink Floyd put out their smash concept album, *The Wall*.

Pat Benatar released *In the Heat of the Night*. Boston Celtics guard Chris Ford scored the first three-point basket in NBA history. Led Zeppelin released their last album before John Bonham succumbed to alcohol poisoning in 1980, and the Eagles released *The Long Run*. Their final album of the 1970s.

Motörhead released their second thrash metal album, *Overkill*. The movie *Rock N' Roll High School*, featuring the Ramones, was released. Frank Zappa brought humor back into music with their seventh studio album, *Sheik Yerbouti*. The B-52s continued the humor with the song "Rock Lobster" from their debut album.

Southern Rock is back as Molly Hatchet releases their second album, Flirtin' *With Disaster, and* Led Zeppelin releases their eighth studio album, *In Through The Out Door*. Chuck Berry began a four-month prison term for tax evasion, and Howard Stern began broadcasting at WCCC in Hartford, Connecticut.

It was also the year I learned my first lead. My playing was about to transition from the plateau stage to the stage of climbing Mount Everest. The southern rock band Blackfoot released the song "Train, Train" that year. The song's lead was likely played with a slide, and the guitar player probably used an open G tuning.

But it was simple, and I could play it without a slide and in standard tuning using bends to emulate the sound of a slide. My finger strength was growing, and it felt easy and natural to play. This was the train that would take me on out of this town.

I had a burning desire to understand the why of music, yet harmony and theory remained a mystery to me. I felt I was finally getting a grip on how the instrument was meant to be played, but I knew there had to be reasons why everything worked the way it did.

There are numerous stories of rock stars making it without understanding how to read music, but understanding harmony and theory is so much more than just recognizing note values on the staff.

Like most high school friends, Billy, Tommy, and I grew apart as high school progressed. We were getting our driver's licenses, and I worked as a cook at a Sonic Burger drive-in restaurant, saving my money to buy a car. I divided my time between working and keeping up with school.

I would still find other guitar players to jam with, but that would usually consist of getting high or tripping on acid, turning our guitars up as loud as they would go, and finding a groove.

Most of my attention was on girls and getting laid. I, like so many other young males, masturbated in the shower so frequently that every time it rained, my dick got hard.

If we weren't thinking or talking about girls, we were getting high, drinking alcohol, and cruising Main Street. We talked about girls we saw in Playboy magazine or told stories of things we had done to girls in the past. All bullshit, of course, but a passage to manhood nonetheless.

Schools Out

On February 19th in the year of our Lord, 1980, Bon Scott, the lead singer for AC/DC, died after passing out from alcohol intoxication. He choked to death on his own vomit. By July 25th, Brian Johnson had replaced Bon as the lead singer, and they released their critically acclaimed album *Back in Black*. Rock n' roll mourned no one. "Ride On," Bon, "Ride On."

On February 22nd, the United States Hockey team defeated the Soviet Union in the semi-finals at the XIII Winter Olympics in Lake Placid, New York. Iron Maiden released their self-titled debut album. Motörhead pounded out their fifth album, *Ace of Spades,* and Judas

Priest released their sixth album, *British Steel*, featuring the songs "Breaking the Law" and "Living After Midnight."

Ozzy Osbourne found a new guitarist named Randy Rhoads, who showcased his guitar mastery on the album *Blizzard of Ozz*. Meanwhile, Ozzy's old band, Black Sabbath, refused to be outdone, releasing *Heaven and Hell* with their new lead singer, Ronny James Dio.

On May 18th, Mount Saint Helens in Washington State erupted, killing more than fifty people. Rush became more commercial with *Permanent Waves*. Van Halen released their third album with David Lee Roth. Molly Hatchet continued their run with *Beatin' the Odds*, and Journey's *On Through the Night* marked their third album with Steve Perry.

Pop rock was making its mark with Pat Benatar's release of *Crimes of Passion*. Dire Straits was serenading us with "Romeo and Juliet" on their third album, *Making Movies*. Def Leppard said "Hello America" on the release of their debut album, *On Through the Night*, and Huey Lewis and the News released their self-titled album.

New wave was permeating the radio as INXS, The Pretenders, and The Romantics released their debut albums. Devo, The Police, Talking Heads, and The Cars released their third albums. Blondie released their fifth album, *Autoamerican*, featuring the song "Call Me."

Gothic began with The Cure's release of their second album, *Seventeen Seconds*. The Rockers of the sixties refused to be forgotten when Jeff Beck released his masterpiece *There and Back*, and technology continued its steady march when the Pac-Man video game made its way into arcades around the country.

It was also the year I turned eighteen and graduated from high school. Mark would be eleven at the end of the year, and my premonition of early disaster disappeared as he turned into a pretty cool little human.

He was developing a sense of humor, loved listening to my old records, and enjoyed watching me play the guitar. We shared a love for music and spent a lot of time together exploring that common ground.

For most of the kids in my class, it was just another summer break before they went to college. For those of us who couldn't afford or didn't want to go to college, we were looking for a job and a way to support ourselves.

I landed a job at a music store in the city, which was a suburb of my town. It took about forty-five minutes to drive to work every day, but it was worth it.

Rock City Music Center was one of the largest music stores in the city. Not only did I meet a multitude of musicians, but I also perfected the fine art of guitar maintenance and set-up. I would never allow anyone to touch my guitar again. It was a dream job.

Jeffrey "Guitar" Holten and I were in the guitar department, selling guitars and amps. Despite being close to thirty, he still had a youthful look and outlook on life. He was a jazz cat who played parties in the ritzy parts of the city.

His band would read charts and play jazz standards, as well as the top 40 tunes of the day. No rehearsal. Just show up and read charts. They would collect a couple hundred bucks a night each for their trouble and expertise. This was between two and four times the amount a musician in the bars received.

Jeff was prodigious and had been playing his entire life. He knew the importance of maintaining his own guitars and taught me how to re-string a guitar with a wrap on the top of the tuning peg to prevent it from slipping out of tune.

He also taught me how to intonate a guitar so every note rang true across the entire neck. The Rocky Roller guys had started me on the maintenance quest, and Jeff gave me the final pieces.

There were two sides to Jeff. Jeff the guitar tech and Jeff the player. Jeff, the player, could play anything. When it was slow in the store, we would "test" the equipment. He would teach me chordal progressions and licks that kept me busy every night.

He loved playing the music of Edgar Winter, Jimi Hendrix, Creedence Clearwater Revival, Stevie Wonder, and the standards of the late 1960s and early 1970s. Jeff was a bluesman at heart. He played jazz to make a living. That in itself was ironic. He got to do the one thing in life he loved the most, but had to whore himself out to a style that, even though more technical and complex, wasn't his passion.

He would play Edgar Winter's song "Free Ride" or one of his seventh and ninth chord progressions. I would turn down my guitar and watch intently, trying to follow the chords he played. I learned so much from him, and when he broke into his technical skills, all I could do was smile and watch him play.

After a few months of working on what I learned during the day, I could jam with him. I could hold down the rhythm while he played leads on top of it, and he would return the favor by doing the same for me. I was coming into my own as a player, and he must have been pleased with the impact and influence he was having on me.

We became fast friends, and sometimes, when he would walk around the store, he would sing the old Bobby Goldsboro song, "Watching Scotty Grow." It was quite hilarious, and he made me feel like I was becoming the best guitar player in the city. His acceptance made me feel extraordinary.

Jimmy was the drum guy and played in one of the most popular reggae bands in the city. He was a white guy who loved reggae and had the chops to play with some of the best in his genre.

He had long, blondish-brown hair and blue eyes. He would often have Rastafarians from Jamaica staying at his house as they passed through our state, playing the bar circuit.

I remember him being quiet and staying to himself, but when he demonstrated the drum kits, his timing was unwavering, and his drum chops would have rivaled anyone's. He also had connections to some of the best weed in the city and didn't have a problem supplying me and Jeff.

Doug was the manager and keyboard guy. He spent most of his time in the office doing paperwork, but sometimes, he would come onto the sales floor.

There was always a cigarette in his mouth when he walked over to a synthesizer or electric piano. He would talk to a client with that cigarette hanging in his mouth and the smoke wafting into the air. How it didn't blow into his eyes, I will never know.

He would play some fantastic riffs and then let the client show what they had. He would find an ashtray for the long ash on his smoke and push buttons, demonstrating the features and sounds.

It always ended with Doug writing up an order. He would walk them back to the counter, take their money, give them their new toy, shake their hand, and return to his office. It was really something to behold.

One day, I got a call from a guy inquiring about a new Roland drum machine we had just received. I assured him we had it in stock and asked if he wanted me to set it aside. He told me he was doing a gig a few cities away and offered me backstage passes to his show if I brought it to him. It turned out he was the drummer for Eddie Money, and they were backing up ZZ Top.

After work, Jeff, Jimmy, and I would go to the clubs to check out the local bands and try to drum up some business. There were two major clubs in town. The drinking age for three point two percent beer was eighteen, and the club that served only three point two percent beer was called LT's Nightclub.

The club that served six percent beer and hard alcohol was located in the building next to it. It was called Impala's Lounge. It was literally a two-minute walk from the front door of one to the front door of the other.

LT's had local bands, but Impala's had the touring bands, which were the best bands around the country. Every night we went out, Jimmy and Jeff would leave me at LT's when they went to Impala's. I had to get into that club.

With Jimmy's help, I found a guy who made fake IDs. It cost me a hundred bucks, but he guaranteed me it would work. After I received it, I couldn't contain my excitement, so I decided to try it out and ventured out alone.

As I entered Impala's, I was surprised that no one checked my ID, so I kept it in my top pocket, anticipating the need. There was a wall of amps on the stage, and the band was blaring out the hits of the day.

The band's break began as soon as I walked to the bar. I walked to the stage, introduced myself, and handed one of my business cards to the guitarist. He smiled as we shook hands, and he introduced himself as Jett Starr. Not his real name, of course, but a stage name. I'll never forget that name. Two Ts, two Rs. I had to get me a stage name.

Jett was a cool guy who liked to talk and was eager to show me the secrets of a touring bar band. I stepped onto the stage with him, and he pointed out that all the amps, aside from the ones they played through, were made of cardboard. The entire wall of sound was nothing but a facade. I never looked at stage set-ups the same again.

I walked to the bar and ordered a beer. The bartender asked me for my ID. I smiled and looked him in the eye as I pulled out the fake one and handed it to him.

He looked at the ID, then at me, and finally back at the picture on the document. He looked back up at me, put the ID in his pocket, and signaled one of the bouncers to come to the bar.

He whispered into the bouncer's ear, and I was escorted out of the bar. On the way out, they informed me that if I came back, they would call the police.

I had only watched this band play half of a song, and from what I heard, I wanted to see more. Dejected, I returned to LT's to drown my sorrows. That's when I met Penny.

Penny was a waitress in the bar and stood at my table, asking me what I wanted to drink. She had brown eyes, long blonde hair, and a body to kill for. I didn't have much luck with the ladies, but her smile and demeanor captivated me.

I was amazed she found me attractive and interesting enough to talk to. For me, it was love at first sight, and before I knew it, we were in the back seat of my car, making out and getting more intimate. Little cars suck for making out, and it was only a matter of time before we were meeting at her sister's house or anywhere we could be alone.

She was my first love, and I fell for her hard. All I could think about was being with her. I was willing to give up music, settle down, and work a regular job for the rest of my life just so I could wake up where she was every morning.

Being with her became an obsession. I couldn't concentrate at work. I couldn't eat, sleep, or play guitar. The only thing I could do was think about her. It seemed I was meant for her, and she was meant for me.

After work, I grabbed Penny, and we jumped into my car to drive to the show I was invited to with the new drum machine in hand. I didn't get to meet Eddie Money or any of the members of ZZ Top, but I spent at least an hour talking to Eddie Money's guitar player. I was amazed by his humility and the time he took to talk to me.

He told me about life on the road and complained about how his guitar tech couldn't tune a guitar. He was definitely extraordinary, and I remembered why I wanted to be a rock star.

I stood in awe, watching him, Eddie Money, and ZZ Top play their sets as the behind-the-scenes activities unfolded around me. I learned so much that night, and it helped me create a plan for how I could marry Penny and still pursue my music.

On the drive home, Penny informed me that her parents were out of town, and I could spend the night with her. The night just kept getting better.

When we got to her house, it was late. By the time we walked through the door, we were both so hot that we used the pull-out couch to make love and eventually fall asleep.

Early in the morning, there was a knock on the door. After a few seconds, the door opened. "Oh, hi, Grandma," Penny said nervously in my dream.

"Looks like you had a friend sleep over," Grandma replied as she walked toward the bed, looking at Penny and trying to see through my blanket-covered face and body.

My hairy and obviously male leg was sticking out of the blanket, and I couldn't get it covered fast enough. Grandma walked to my side of the bed, throwing the covers off and exposing our naked bodies and my undeniable maleness. Penny went into a frenzy, yelling and crying, but her Grandmother stayed focused on me.

I sat at the edge of the bed, putting on my clothes as Grandma screamed in my face, shaking a finger at me. I was in shock, and although I could see her lips move, I couldn't hear what she was saying.

There was no way I was going to get into a pissing match with an old lady, so I finished getting dressed and walked to my car with Grandma close behind.

She continued her rant, and I could feel and see her rage as I closed the car door. I'm pretty sure she woke up everyone in the neighborhood, but I was oblivious and just wanted to make my escape.

I never saw Penny again. I tried calling, and I went to her house. Each time, her parents or her grandmother turned me away. All my pleading and crying would do nothing to change their minds. I went to her work and was told she had quit the same day her grandmother had caught us in the makeshift bed.

I staked out her house and sat in my car all weekend, hoping for a glimpse of her. I was gutted. I truly wanted to die. My weight loss was noticeable, and I couldn't live without her. I just wanted to sleep and cry.

At a different time, I would have continued my quest to get her back. I would have waited for her forever and found her, no matter where she was on earth.

But for some reason, this had the opposite effect. Being abandoned had taught me that fighting only caused more heartache and that no matter how hard you cried, they weren't coming back.

I buried my head in my studies with Jeff, trying to work away my broken heart. I justified my actions by convincing myself that I could have a thousand girls better than Penny when I was the rock star I was destined to be.

I vowed that I would never be tied down to just one girl again. I was more determined than ever to become the best guitar player in the world and to climb to the top. The pain never went away, but with time, it subsided.

White Lines

MTV launched in 1981, airing music videos twenty-four hours a day. ZZ Top dominated MTV's airwaves with the release of *El Loco*, featuring "Tube Snake Boogie" and "Pearl Necklace." The J. Geils Band also took advantage of the heavy rotation they received on MTV with their album *Freeze Frame*.

Tom Petty continued showing his top-ten hit-writing prowess with the release of *Hard Promises*. Van Halen continued to amaze with his never-ending licks and musical genius with the release of *Fair Warning*, and April Wine hit commercial success with the album *The Nature of the Beast*.

Ozzy Osbourne continued to be propelled by Randy Rhoads' guitar wizardry with the release of *"Diary of a Madman."* It was the last album Randy would perform on. During the North American leg of the tour for the album, a small plane he was riding in clipped Ozzy's tour bus and crashed, causing his untimely death. He was twenty-five.

Ozzy's former band, Black Sabbath, continued its success with Ronny James Dio and the album *Mob Rules*. AC/DC released its second album with Brian Johnson, *For Those About to Rock*, and Joan Jett released the songs "Bad Reputation" and "I Love Rock N' Roll."

Foreigner found success with their album *4,* while Phil Collins released his first solo album, *Face Value*. Mötley Crüe and Dokken released their debut albums, and Rush continued its mainstream success with *Moving Pictures*.

The Rolling Stones released *Tattoo You*, and Stevie Nicks released *Bella Donna*. Heavy Metal continued its march with Iron Maiden releasing its second album, *Killers*, and Saxon, the band credited with influencing Metallica and Mötley Crüe, released their fourth album, *Denim and Leather*.

It was also the year Ryan walked into Rock City Music Center, and my life would be altered in ways I never imagined. The sun was at an angle that day, allowing its rays to penetrate deep into the store.

As he entered the door, the sun's rays glowed around him, showing only a silhouette of his body. He looked like a bad guy on the prairie in a cheap spaghetti western.

Jimmy greeted him as he walked to the drum section and then disappeared into the back, leaving Ryan at the glass display case in his area. Jimmy returned with two Zildjian cymbals that Ryan had previously special-ordered. Ryan was a drummer, and he had money to burn.

He was back in the store a few days later, putting the finishing touches on his kit. Then he returned a few weeks after that and purchased a tri-amp PA system that could have filled any club in town with sound. He was forming a band and approached me about being the lead guitarist.

I must admit, I felt a little intimidated by all the expensive equipment he was purchasing. However, it would give me an opportunity to meet more musicians and work on my chops, so I agreed to meet with him and jam with his band.

Turned out Ryan was one of the largest cocaine dealers in the city. Life was about to become more complicated, and Penny would soon become a distant memory. I arrived at a two-story house larger than it appeared from the outside and pounded on the door.

I could see the kitchen and dining room as I walked into the entryway. To my left, a stairway descended to a lower level where the band was set up. Standing at the bottom of the stairs was another guitar player named Sam.

Dave, the bass player, stood next to Sam, and Ryan sat behind his drums, smiling as I walked down the stairs. The 16-channel board he purchased from Jimmy the week before was in the back of the room.

Next to the board sat a road case containing three power amplifiers and an equalizer. Wires ran out of the biggest power amp and into the end-table-sized subwoofer cabinets.

The remaining power amps had the same cords running to the mid and treble cabinets, which sat on top of the subwoofers, one on top of another.

At the front of the room, microphones had been set up in front of everyone, with an extra one positioned in the empty space where my amp would fit perfectly. Ryan had spent a considerable amount of time and money putting this together and ensuring I felt accepted.

My feelings of insecurity crept in, and I wondered if I would be qualified to play with these guys. Looking at the mic made me feel even more insecure. I never considered myself a singer and had always concentrated on playing guitar.

I set my amp in the empty space and plugged it into the wall. The room was silent, and I could feel everyone's eyes upon me. I pulled my old Les Paul from the case, strapped it on, and plugged it into a tuner. Satisfied it was in tune, I plugged it into my amplifier.

My heart started beating faster as the memories of puking my guts out in front of everyone at the high school party passed through my mind. I excused myself and ran to the bathroom, expelling the lunch I had eaten earlier.

When I returned, Ryan was cutting up lines of cocaine on a mirror, and Sam was rolling a joint. They passed the mirror around, and Ryan ensured I was first in line. I picked up a golden tube lying on the mirror, lightly put it in my nose, and sniffed the white powder, feeling an immediate rush.

My stomach settled, and I felt re-energized. I hit the joint, strapped on my guitar, and turned the volume up on my amp. "What's the band's name?" I asked.

"White Lines," they responded simultaneously.

Cool, I thought as I smashed a power chord and let it ring before laying my fingers on the fretboard, stopping the sound. Sam smiled, and Ryan counted us in.

We jammed on some easy songs of the day. "Cocaine" by Eric Clapton, "Paranoid" by Black Sabbath, and "Breaking the Law" by Judas Priest were some of the tunes we all knew.

We were about the same skill level, and Dave, the other guitarist, didn't want to play lead, so I played them all. I also sang that night, which I never thought I would do.

The jam went well, and we seemed to mesh as people, so when Ryan and the boys offered me a bedroom upstairs if I could pay one-fifth of the rent, I agreed. I quickly found myself living in an out-of-control band house with no parental supervision.

We all had day jobs except for Ryan. Sam and Dave worked in construction, and I continued working at the music store with a much shorter drive time. We would get high and jam every evening when everyone returned from work.

Living in my first band house was about what you'd expect. The drugs flowed freely, there was always alcohol to drink, and beautiful women came by every night to keep us company and watch us play. Groupies come in all forms, from the amateur to the professional, and these girls wanted to be close to the band.

None of us had girlfriends. What was the sense? The combination of coke, weed, and alcohol brought in girls from far and wide. I got laid more while living in that house than I ever thought possible. I even experienced my first threesome. Life was good.

We never jammed late during the week as we all had to get up early for work, but our jams would get out of control on the weekends. "Tell them to fuck off," Ryan would scream when the police showed up at the door because of complaints from the neighbors.

My room was across the hall from Ryan's, and I had to pass his door to get to my room. Almost every time I walked out of my room, he had a line of his newest shipment cut up on his mirror. "Hey, come in here for a minute," he would yell as I walked by. "I just got a new batch, and I want you to tell me if it's any good."

He claimed he didn't do his own stash, and I can honestly say I never saw him snort a line of coke in all the time I knew him. I found out later that sitting in a closet by himself, sticking a needle in his arm, and shooting it directly into his veins was how he chose to ride his white horse.

Ryan announced that another of his friends would be moving into the house with us. The house had a basement about the size of a bedroom, and he decided a girl named Shelly would move into it.

Shelly was a stunning redhead who was one of Danny's dealers. She loved listening to the band play, and during an off night, she and I sat down to play a game of cards. The conversation became sexual, and I challenged her to a game where the loser would have to do whatever the winner asked.

I considered myself a skilled card player, and she agreed to my terms. I thought I played the best game of my life, but later found out she let me win.

Later that night, Shelly woke me up, holding her finger to her lips and signaling me to be quiet. She stepped back from the bed and slowly did a striptease, trying to keep her private parts covered with her hands. It was one of the most erotic things I had ever seen.

She dropped her hands for a few seconds, allowing me to gaze at her naked body, and jumped into bed. She pulled the covers over herself and curled up next to me. I have to admit that I was both shocked and pleased that she had chosen me for her rendezvous. The sex was incredible, and when I woke up the next day, she was gone.

We never spoke about it again. I thought about starting a relationship with her and even tried hooking up with her again. She always shut me down quickly and returned to whatever it was she was doing.

It was embarrassing and a blow to my ego, but Ryan supplied her business, and she thought it was better that no one knew about our night together. She was busy dealing drugs and making money, and I was busy adhering to my three-foot rule. Any girl who got within three feet of me, I was trying to fuck. She had just been lucky enough to be in that circle.

Shelly became my go-to dealer and friend after that night. We had sex a couple more times during our one-sided relationship, but my stopping by for fifteen to thirty minutes and then leaving was the norm. Reloading my stash and catching up on her life was about as close as we ever got. It never seemed she was interested in me, and the magic I felt that first night faded.

Ryan continued to entice me into his room with lines of cocaine daily. It continued for the first few weeks of my residency and then suddenly stopped. One day, I slowly walked by his room, waiting for him to invite me in, but he never even looked my way.

I started feeling a little paranoid, thinking I had done something to upset him. A line sounded good, so I walked into his room and asked if everything was okay. He assured me it was.

"You want to cut up a line? I could use a little bump." I blurted out, not realizing how much I'd grown dependent on the substance.

"Oh, that shit's not free," was his answer.

My stomach dropped as the words sank in, and I realized how badly I needed a line. "How much is it?"

"Hundred dollars a gram." He calmly said, "And if you buy in quantity, I can give it to you for less."

"It's alright, man, I don't get paid until Friday, so I can catch you then."

"Wait a minute," he quickly responded. "I'll tell you what. I'll front it to you, and you can pay me when you get paid."

I was being set up by a drug dealer, and it didn't take long for my bill to grow. He never gave a weekly tally, and I never thought of keeping track of how much I received.

A couple of months after our discussion, Ryan approached me again. "You owe me three grand, and I can't front anymore to you until it's paid."

My heart sank to my stomach, and the blood left my face. I couldn't believe I did over an ounce of blow in such a short time. I was in trouble and had visions of Ryan taking my guitars and amps to satisfy my debt.

I soon found out my fears were unfounded and that Sam and Dave had fallen into the same trap well before me. They had been dealing in the clubs for him since I moved in, and it looked like I would suffer the same fate. But he had something else in mind for me.

"Sam and Dave, help me out by collecting money I'm owed," he stated. "Why don't you join them for the night, and I can cut what you owe me by a few hundred dollars?"

Fuck...I didn't want to go to jail or get shot trying to collect money for his amusement. I was nineteen and enjoying my freedom. But I knew the bill had to be paid. "I don't carry," I heard myself say.

"That's fine," he quickly responded. "You can be the mouthpiece, and Sam and Dave will take care of the rest."

I didn't think I had a massive habit, and I could have quit any time I wanted, but the girls loved it, and well, at that age, getting laid was worth the consequences, so I went back for more. At the rate I was going, I would owe him for the rest of my life.

Collection night rolled around, and I found myself sitting in the back of a limousine with Sam on one side of me and Dave on the other. The car stopped. Sam and Dave got out, banged on the front door of a house, and yanked some poor soul to the car.

They roughed him up a little on the way, pushing him to the ground and kicking him. After some screaming and yelling, they picked him up and gently placed him in the back with me.

"It seems we have a problem," I began in my best Godfather imitation. "I want to inform you that you have thirty days to get us the money we are owed, or we will take drastic actions against you and your family." I paused for dramatic effect. "I would hate to see something terrible happen to that beautiful family of yours, so be timely with your payment."

I stared him down, showing we meant business, and motioned to Sam and Dave, who pulled him out of the car and beat the shit out of him again. They dragged him off the shoulder of the road and into the ditch beside it. They got back in the car, and we drove away.

It was hokey. It felt like being in a bad movie, and I wasn't feeling good about myself for being a part of it. We were pretty boys, not thugs.

Suddenly, red lights popped on behind us. *Fuck*, I thought as the blood rushed from my head, and a coldness overtook me. An image of the three of us sitting in jail flashed in my mind.

The limo driver turned around. "Not a word from any of you," he screamed. "Let me do the talking, and you do what you're told. Play it cool, and we might get out of this."

He rolled down the window and handed the officer his license and car registration as they spoke. The back window rolled down, and I could feel my heart pounding through my chest.

The scene unfolded with an eerie familiarity as the officer put his head inside the car and asked for our IDs. He carefully scanned the area where we were sitting, pausing briefly as he took each of our licenses in hand and looked each of us in the eye.

He walked to his car and got in, sitting there for what seemed like forever. My heart continued to pound as I held my breath and sat motionless, watching him walk back to our car.

"Make sure you get that taillight fixed, or next time, I'll give you a ticket," he said, handing the chauffeur his driver's license, our driver's licenses, the car registration, and the insurance card. He glanced back at us as he walked to his car. He got in and slowly drove away. We laughed nervously as the driver handed us our IDs, started the car, and drove us home.

I started packing that night and gave Ryan my entire month's paycheck. It really put me in a bind, but I had to get out of that house and away from certain jail time.

I was a musician, a pretty boy, not a criminal. I watched the movie *Scared Straight* and heard the stories of what they do to young, pretty boys like me in prison. I didn't want to experience it.

Ryan never came out of his room when I moved my bed, dressers, and clothes from my room and carried them to the rented moving truck. He didn't so much as pop his head out once, not even when I went downstairs to retrieve my guitars and amp. I felt tears filling my eyes as I climbed into the moving truck, looked back at the house, and drove down the road.

This was one of the earliest life lessons I learned about living on the streets. Everyone, and I mean everyone, will try to take advantage of you.

Not showing weakness was the only way to stop it. To me, weakness equaled emotion. I vowed never to let my emotions get the better of me again.

It also gave me a taste for cocaine and the party lifestyle that being in a band brought. I was officially hooked. Not only on the new drug I had come to rely on but on the lifestyle itself.

I loved making music with my friends. I loved the party that came with it, and I loved all the women I was able to sleep with. I couldn't even remember what Penny looked like.

I would never look back on the occupation I chose again. Making music was my life. Becoming a rock star and being extraordinary were no longer options. They were now a necessity.

The Party Crew

1982 was a fantastic year for metal. It was an abysmal year for Hollywood. John Belushi, an icon and comedy genius, died from speedballing heroin and cocaine at the age of thirty-three.

Iron Maiden released *The Number of the Beast*. The Scorpions released *Blackout*. Kiss was still rocking with *Creatures of the Night*, and Sammy Hagar released his seventh album, *Three Lock Box*.

Steven Spielberg's *E.T., the Extra-Terrestrial*, was the smash movie of the year. Jimi Hendrix's posthumous fame grew with the release of *The Jimi Hendrix Concerts*. Missing Persons added to its fan base with the release of *Spring Sessions M*. George Thorogood was being "Bad to the Bone," and Rush continued being mainstream with the release of *Signals*.

Van Halen released *Diver Down*. Billy Squier released *Emotion in Motion*, and Pat Benatar released her fourth album, *Get Nervous*. Walt Disney opened its second theme park in Disney World, located in Orlando, Florida, called EPCOT Center, and Robert Plant made his solo debut with *Pictures at Eleven*.

The Jam is happening in the United Kingdom. John Cougar, soon to be known as John Cougar Mellencamp, releases the album *American Fool*, featuring the songs "Hurts So Good" and "Jack and Diane." Night Ranger released its debut album, *Dawn Patrol,"* featuring an 8-finger guitar technique on the song "Rock In America" and the smash hit "Don't Tell Me You Love Me."

Prince released his smash, *1999*. Twisted Sister released their first album, and punk was taking root in California and New York with bands like Fear, The Vandals, and The Dead Kennedys.

Technology took another step when Commodore International released the Commodore 64 personal computer, marking the beginning of the computer craze, and Led Zeppelin released their ninth and final studio album, *Coda*.

I was fired from Rock City Music Center soon after giving Ryan my last month's pay. Before that fateful day, I got to watch Rush from backstage. The backup band was Rory Gallagher, and one of his guitar players needed strings. Rock stars were so extraordinary that they would order out even for something as small as guitar strings.

I paid for the strings out of my pocket and told him not to worry about it. I remember the green room they hung out in, the food, and all of them being very kind and accommodating. But most of all, I remember watching Rush put on an amazing twenty-four-song set.

Looking back on it, this was the best job I ever had. Imagine trying out new guitars, amplifiers, and effects pedals every day. When the store was slow, being schooled by an extraordinary player and receiving free backstage passes to big-name shows.

Unfortunately, by that time, I had become numb and disillusioned and didn't know where to turn. Without a job or money, I had few options and moved back in with my Mother, Ken, and Mark. I had found a new low.

I sat around the house, bong in hand, for a few weeks, wondering why I never saw Ken. Mom started commenting about me getting a job and paying for food, so I decided it was time to return to the workforce. I had no idea what to do.

I had a choice. Cut my hair and start as a salesperson in a shopping mall or leave it long and get a job as a laborer. I chose the laborer's job. It was a hard job that involved a lot of heavy carrying and digging.

But the guys that bossed me around were pretty cool, and they didn't seem to mind when I snuck off to smoke a bowl or do a line. They taught me about the fine art of carpentry and the skills of household repairs.

Work ended for me at six. They might stay on the job longer, but once it was six, I was gone. The great part of being a laborer is there's nothing to learn. When work was over, it was over. My off time was mine, and I could concentrate on music.

The best part of being a laborer was that it paid well. I upgraded my guitars and amps and gave my mom the money she wanted for food. I also continued working on music with Mark and became increasingly amazed by the unique quality of his voice.

Shelly became my exclusive dealer, and the more money I made, the bigger my habit grew. I found a nose spray called Afrin and used it to cover up my habit. I soon found myself addicted to that as well. After upgrading my guitars and amp, it was time to find a new place and be back on my own.

I started going back into Rocky Roller and was reading advertisements on the bulletin board. I found an ad from an established local cover band named "The Party Crew" that was auditioning guitar players. A new chapter in my playing career was about to begin.

I nervously called the number from the small piece of paper I tore off the ad, and after some pleasantries with the band's leader, we set up a day for an audition.

I lugged my new Marshall half-stack down the stairs of my new apartment and placed it in the back of my 1975 Ford Pinto. I headed back upstairs for my main axe, a blue Charvel Model 4 with a 9-volt battery preamp, and my trusty gold-top Les Paul, which I had purchased while working at Rock City.

I ran back up the stairs to grab my effects pedal box, microphone, and microphone stand, as well as my bag full of chords, power supplies, and other miscellaneous gear.

I jumped in the car and soon found myself in a basement with Liam, the band's leader, guitarist, and vocalist. Jerry, the bass player, sang most of the backup vocals, and John, the drummer, was known to sing a song or two.

We exchanged small talk as I set my Marshall head on top of the 4x12 cabinet and connected them. Liam had asked me to learn four songs before the audition. I think they were "Three Steps" by Lynyrd Skynyrd, "Born to be Wild" by Steppenwolf, "The Theme to Peter Gunn," written by Henri Mancini for a private eye show that ran from 1958 to 1961, and "Rock-n-Roll All Night" by Kiss.

I asked where the bathroom was and emptied my stomach as quietly as I could, priming myself with a line. After we played the songs Liam asked me to learn, he asked if I knew any others. I was getting pretty good with Ted Nugent, Led Zeppelin, and Jimi Hendrix tunes, but the first thing that came to mind was the jam sessions I used to have with Jonathan, as well as Tommy and Billy.

I started playing a standard I-IV-V blues progression in A, and they quickly followed the progression I was laying down. We traded off playing lead and rhythm, incorporating drum and bass solo breaks, which allowed everyone time to stretch out and showcase their abilities. Playing with guys this seasoned was incredible, and I was thankful for the opportunity.

I didn't think I played well that night, but I felt I had improved more than I had in all my time living with Ryan in the band house. Liam must have enjoyed it as well. While packing my equipment, he looked at me and said, "Congratulations, you're our new guitar player."

John and Jerry nodded in approval and extended their hands, smiling. We shared a doobie, and as I was leaving, Liam handed me two cassette tapes that contained forty-five minutes of music on each side.

"These are the forty songs we play. We have a gig in two weeks. Rehearsals are on Wednesday and Friday at seven and Saturday at twelve. Don't be late."

I was stunned and looked at him with a half-shit-eating grin, wondering if he was kidding. I looked at his face and then at the tapes he placed in my hand. Forty songs? Two weeks?

How am I going to learn forty songs in two weeks? I thought as I smiled at Liam and looked at John and Jerry. "That's great," I heard myself say. "No problem at all. I'll be here Saturday."

John helped me carry my equipment to my car. "Don't worry about it," he said, sensing my distress at the task I had just been given. "Forty songs isn't so hard to learn, man. Most of them are just standard blues progressions. Once you get a few of them, you have them all."

He smiled and tapped me on the shoulder. "Just remember that this is Liam's band. Don't try to change anything. We'll never play originals, and he's stern about the songs we play. But he's a great guy, and he'll give you some leeway. You're about to learn a lot from one of the masters who's been doing this for years. Enjoy the ride."

I climbed into the driver's seat of my car and looked at the cases containing the tapes I had been given. They were full of songs from the sixties, seventies, and eighties. We started each night with songs like John Cougar's "I Need a Lover" or Tom Petty's "American Girl."

We would move into dance tunes like "Cocaine" from Clapton, "Gimme Three Steps," from Lynyrd Slynyrd, and "Born to Be Wild" from Steppenwolf.

From there, we would start getting harder with Blue Öyster Cult's "ME-262," Black Sabbath's "Paranoid," Led Zeppelin's "*Rock-n-*

Roll," Judas Priest's "Breaking the Law," Van Halen's "Aint Talkin Bout Love," and, well, you get an idea of what the next two weeks would hold in store for me if I was going to pull this off.

I was already practicing my "Why I couldn't do it" speech, which I planned to give to Levi at the next rehearsal, as I pulled into my community parking lot. "I'm sorry, Liam, but..." I practiced in my head as I lugged my equipment up the stairs.

The following two weeks went fast. Other than going to work, I didn't leave my apartment. Cassette tapes were a popular medium for sharing music. Creating a mixtape of songs that held meaning for you and then giving it to a new flame or someone you were courting was a common practice.

Before I was eighteen, I would take the needle of a record player, lift it up, and put it an eighth of an inch behind where it was. Essentially, I created a loop to listen to difficult passages repeatedly until I could emulate what they were doing.

Now, it was possible to press play, listen to a passage, press rewind, then play, and repeatedly listen to the same ten seconds. Fostex released a 4-track cassette recorder called the X-15 with a pitch controller the following year.

With the X-15, I could tune the song to my guitar instead of tuning my guitar to the song. It also allowed me to record four guitar, drum, vocal, and/or bass tracks on a blank cassette tape. It was a dream for aspiring guitar players and songwriters.

Before I left Rock City Music Center, Tom Schultz from the band Boston released a tone-changing guitar practice tool. He called it a Rockman headphone amplifier, and it gave my guitar a heavy metal tone that sounded like the tone he used for his band.

It also had an auxiliary input, allowing me to plug a cassette player into it. I was the only one who could hear the guitar and the song I was trying to learn.

I could practice at two in the morning and not worry about the neighbors calling the cops. Once I got in tune with the recording, it was amazing how fast I could learn the songs.

I didn't have time to learn the leads to the songs note for note, and my philosophy at the time was that if I learned the first few beginning notes, some middle notes, and the end notes correctly, no one would notice the rest was practiced improvisation.

I plugged my new Rockman into my Walkman and tuned the guitar to the song. I sat on the couch, bong in hand, with the television playing some stupid T&A movie I rented from the local video store. I hit stop, rewind, play, stop, rewind, and play over and over, trying to match the notes on my guitar with what I heard on the tape.

When I got lost, I would rewind the song to the beginning and play it to the problem area, then repeat the process. As the two-week mark approached, I could play all the songs Liam had given me.

Rehearsals were long and tedious, but Liam was open to changing a song's arrangement and accepted my partly improvised leads. Some of the songs he wanted to play were out of his vocal range, so I quickly learned to transpose a song to a different key. We were a "raw" band. Not quite as "raw" as a garage band, but not as polished as a touring band. It was one of our biggest draws.

Liam was a perfectionist when it came to arranging the songs and the stage show we performed. We played the same song repeatedly until he was satisfied with both the song and the choreography. We made no major mistakes, had the songs down, and covered all the nuances. We also smoked a lot of weed and consumed excessive amounts of alcohol during practice. It made the time go by and prepared me for the club scene.

The Grand Illusion

The night of our first gig was upon us. Just as it had during our school project, my stomach twisted and turned every time I thought about playing in front of people. The memory of throwing up and passing out at what I now affectionately referred to as the puke party still haunted me. I believed I gave myself a severe illness with the combination of shrooms and Wild Turkey that night, and I thought I was going to die because of it.

Dying young was the dream of the stars, and I had accepted my fate if it meant being extraordinary. James Dean said it best before he died in 1955. "To live fast, die young, and leave a beautiful corpse." It was a quote from the book "*Knock on Any Door*," written by Willard Motley in 1947. In my opinion, as well as James Dean's, it summed up the life of the extraordinary.

We met at our practice house and loaded our equipment. I declined to get high or drink the beer in Liam's refrigerator, telling them my nerves were getting the best of me.

Jerry's PA had a power amp/effects case that was about four feet tall. It had a huge 1500-watt power amp for the lows, an 800-watt power amp for the mids, and a 400-watt power amp for the highs. There was also a separate reverb, delay, and other effects modules inside it. When we put on the front lid, it looked like a refrigerator, but it weighed significantly more. Moving it was awkward, and it took all of us to lift it into the van. When we arrived at the club, it took at least two men to carry it in, and all of us to get it up a flight of stairs.

In addition to "The Refrigerator," the speaker setup was even more massive. The lows held 15-inch woofers and were housed in cabinets that measured about three and a half feet square. It took two men to carry each one. A three-foot-square cabinet housed the mids and their twelve-inch subwoofers. They were lighter but awkward to carry, and also required two men to carry them.

The top held tweeter horns and was about two and a half feet square. They were the lightest and easiest to carry. All of the speaker cabinets had handles on the side, so one person could haul both the tweeter horns in one trip. One set of lows, mids, and highs went on each side of the stage.

We had a sixteen-channel mixing console that took two men to carry, and it was positioned either on the stage with us or at the back of the club we were playing. There were microphones, microphone stands, and a vast array of cords that plugged into the mixing console we affectionately called "The Board," and our sound system was complete.

We also had our personal equipment. I had my Marshall head with a cabinet holding four 12-inch speakers. Liam was running a 2x12 Fender Twin Reverb. Jerry had a monster bass rig taller than my half stack, and there were all of John's drums. Two bass drums, a snare drum, two toms, and a floor tom. It took us each two trips to carry in our amplifier cabinets and power heads, and one trip each to get John's drums.

We also had our miscellaneous equipment. Liam, Jerry, and I had our effects pedals, chords, and miscellaneous gear. John had his assortment of Zildjian cymbals, drumsticks, and drum throne.

He packed everything into cases with precision, keeping it all meticulously organized. He tried to make everything easy to carry, so the four of us could haul our pedals and miscellaneous items, as well as his, in one trip each.

Jerry had a white van, and we strategically packed it with the sound system, guitar, bass amps, and drums. The guitars, chords, mics, mic stands, and miscellaneous gear squeezed into my Pinto. It literally took an hour to pack and load everything.

The analog watch on my wrist showed six-thirty. We still needed to drive to the club, unload the equipment, and set it up. Our first set started at nine. I never imagined that playing in a band would be such a demanding job.

The movies of me becoming a rock star and having roadies to move all this shit played in my head. I would show up with fifteen minutes to spare and walk onto the stage to the roar of my adoring fans. The adoration echoed in my ears as I followed the white van down Colorado Boulevard.

We pulled into a parking lot with a sign that read Frank's Bar and Grill. I exited my car and trotted, catching up with the rest of the band before they entered the door. It was a nice-looking place. The food looked appetizing, and it appeared to be clean. There was only one problem. I didn't see a stage.

"So where do we set up?" I asked.

Liam looked at me and laughed. "Follow me." We climbed two flights of stairs and entered a room filled with tables and a stage at the far end. "Right over there," he pointed.

You're fucking kidding me, I thought. Working like this wasn't matching the fantasies in my head.

We must have walked up and down those stairs ten times, straining and cussing to get the equipment to the stage. Finally, after what seemed like an endless task, we took one last trip to lock the cars, smoke a joint, and grab any miscellaneous items we missed.

I caught my breath as I stepped onto the stage, lit a cigarette, placed my Marshall head on the speaker cabinet, and started plugging everything in. My arms and legs felt like rubber, and I was already exhausted.

I worked all day as a laborer for a construction company, and now I felt more like a laborer for a moving company than a musician. It was unbelievable how much work this first gig was. I navigated my head through my guitar strap, placed it on my shoulder, and strummed an open A chord. The guitar hung loosely from my shoulder as I kneeled down to look in my bag for an instrument cable and a tuner.

It was eight-thirty, and people were arriving. I placed an unlit cigarette between the strings and headstock of my guitar and quickened my pace. With my guitar still hanging at my side and the tuning just right, I took the cigarette from the headstock and placed it between my lips.

I made my way toward Liam and Jerry, and we all plucked an A note, ensuring we were in tune with one another. John did a few rolls on his drums and broke into a mini-solo to the cheers and amusement of the light crowd.

Our table sat to the right of the stage, where we would sit and drink if we weren't playing or mingling with the crowd. We played four sets and received one free drink per set, so we each received four beers per night. My nerves were going crazy, and I started with water, saving my beers for later that night.

We sat at the table, smoking cigarettes and watching the room fill with smoke. It would be a good night for the till. People always drank more when they had a cigarette between their fingers.

Liam, Jerry, and John made their way into the audience, shaking hands and talking to their fans. Wings started flapping in my stomach, and I ran to the bathroom, making it into a stall just in time. The contents of my stomach spilled into the water of the waiting toilet below me.

This time it seemed worse. My eyes watered, and I felt like they would pop out of my head as I heaved. Visions of a doctor telling me I had an incurable disease played in my mind, and I tried to shake the

121

thought. I heaved again, this time with yellow bile and water coming out.

Sweat formed on my forehead and the back of my neck, and I felt like I was going to pass out. My hands were wet and clammy, and I wondered if I could do this. I dry-heaved a couple more times and wanted to tell Liam I was sick and needed to go home. I walked to the mirror, giving myself self-talk and splashing cold water on my face.

Returning to the stall, I carefully pulled out a rectangular piece of folded magazine paper. *A line always helps me clear my nerves,* I thought.

After rolling up a dollar bill, I placed it above the white powder. I sniffed deeply, inhaling the stimulant into my nasal cavity and lungs. I put the bill to my other nostril and sniffed again.

My stomach calmed, and I sighed a breath of relief. I sat on the toilet for a few seconds, regaining my senses, and exited the stall. I wiped my nose and looked at myself in the mirror as I walked by.

Liam, Jerry, and John were already on the stage, and the place was packed. I walked to the stage, still weak and sweaty from my pilgrimage.

I'm not sure if Liam wandered into the bathroom and heard me vomiting or if he could see the anxiety on my pale, sweaty face. But as I strapped on my guitar, he walked over and placed a revised set list on top of my amp.

"I decided to do our easiest songs this set," he yelled in my ear. "When I did my first gig, I didn't look at anyone for the first few songs. Try that. And hey, don't worry about anything. These people will be drunk in an hour and won't remember how we played tomorrow. Just don't forget—we're here to sell drinks. We're not rock stars."

Yet, I thought as he walked away. His advice re-energized, reminded, and re-centered me on my ultimate goal. I heeded his advice, turned my back to the crowd, and breathed deeply.

I concentrated on the intro to the song we were about to play and looked John in the eye as he counted the tempo. Liam began playing, and I fired into the intro lead. I became focused, and the butterflies flew out of my stomach.

I was always thankful for Liam's kindness that night. He covered me during that first set, and I'm not sure I would have followed through on my commitment without him. After I settled down, I turned around and looked at the crowd. The anxiety passed, and I knew I was going to be okay.

That night taught me more than all the years I spent practicing in my bedroom or playing with White Lines. The first thing it taught me was that, given a deadline to learn forty songs, it's possible to remember them. Without a deadline, I would have sat in my bedroom for years, trying to learn those same forty songs. Deadlines were important.

Second, I could feel myself improving while playing in front of a crowd. I don't know if it was from a desire not to embarrass myself or from feeding off the energy of a large crowd, but I could feel something greater come into my soul. The fingerings almost seemed easier to play, and the groove was easier to find. I relaxed and let go, enjoying the experience.

The third thing I learned was that even though my anxiety would make me throw up before getting on stage, I could calm down after a line of coke. After the first few songs passed, the illness would become a memory. The show must go on, and no matter what, I had to have a great night and play like I had never played before.

Most of our gigs were on Friday and Saturday nights, so we didn't have to lug our equipment back to the band house every night. This was one of those gigs. When I returned home, I did a couple of bong hits, obsessed about the night, and had the rest I deserved.

The second night finished without incident or embarrassment. I still suffered from the throw-ups, but I could feel myself getting more comfortable on stage and improving as an entertainer. We ended the night and started packing our equipment around one-fifteen in the morning.

We lugged our equipment down the two flights of stairs we had hauled it up the night before and loaded it into Jerry's van. Liam called shotgun in the van, and John squeezed into my car. I was still breathing hard as we followed the white van to our practice space.

We unpacked the PA system and John's drums, taking them inside. After unloading the equipment, I climbed into my car and drove home, my ears still ringing from the night. I unpacked my guitars, ran them up the stairs, and returned to my car.

I rolled in the 4x12 cabinet, hauled it up the stairs, and then ran back down, retrieving my Marshall head, pedal board, and a bag of chords. *This is a lot of work,* I thought, gasping for breath. I looked at the clock. It was four a.m.

I climbed into my little car and drove to my parking spot. *Thank God I don't have to work tomorrow.*

I worked harder that weekend than any job I've ever worked and for a lot less money. My body ached, and I knew I would be sore in the morning.

I took a hit from the bong sitting on my table, sat on the couch, and fantasized about roadies hauling the equipment while I hung out in my hotel room doing ungodly things to the babes. I walked to the bathroom, turned on the shower, and undressed. My commitment to my Rock n' Roll Fantasy was stronger than ever before.

Tainted Love

The following Friday came fast, and I found myself back in a strange, shit-smelling public restroom, spewing my guts into an unfamiliar commode.

I expected it this time, but it almost felt worse than the week before. With every extended heave, I leaned over the porcelain nightmare, hoping my eyes wouldn't pop out of my head. My loathing of this unclean ceremony grew with each endured repetition, and I wished it would stop.

I reaffirmed my promise of no alcohol from the week before and wiped my mouth as I walked to the sink. I splashed cold water on my face and washed my hands. Returning to the stall, I snorted a line.

As I walked out of the bathroom, Liam looked up from the stage and smiled. This club looked like the one we played the weekend before, except it didn't, thank God, have stairs.

I stepped onto the stage. "It'll get better," Liam said as I walked by. I forced a smile, strapped on my guitar, squirted some Afrin up each nostril, and started the tuning process of my guitars.

After the first set, one of the Mikes made a surprise visit. He talked me into going outside during our second break to smoke a doobie and do a quick line. I hadn't seen him in a long time and wanted to catch up, so I agreed.

The band took fifteen-minute breaks after each forty-five-minute set, so I didn't have much time. We ran to Mike's car, and I lit a pipe he handed me as he cut up a line. After snorting the lines on the mirror and taking another hit from the pipe, we ran back into the bar.

Liam started playing the introduction to Billy Idol's White Wedding. I was late. I was high. And I was hyperventilating from the run. Jerry's bass was trying to cover up my missing part.

I quickly strapped on my guitar, still hyperventilating with my heart pounding. Liam, Jerry, and John all stopped playing. My guitar solo was intended to break the silence and end the interlude.

Instead, my mind went blank. I froze and looked at the audience, reaching the same anxiety level and embarrassment I felt at the puke party. Liam looked at me with disappointment and played a simple lead, trying to cover my mistake.

Missing the lead was embarrassing enough. Seeing the disappointment on Liam's face was devastating. I was never late again.

After the song, Liam joked to the audience that his guitar player was stoned out of his mind and invited the crowd to do the same. I thought I would get fired, but he never said anything more about it.

I knew I'd fucked up, and Liam knew I knew. He was a consummate professional, and his band was the first one I gigged with in clubs. I hated knowing I had let him down, and I was grateful that he was a partier who remembered his beginnings. I owed him a lot.

As we went on our second break, I noticed a girl in the audience laughing with all her friends. It was Rachel Conrad. The most beautiful girl in school.

Her family had moved into our area when I was in the seventh grade, and I remembered the first time I saw her. The Mikes and I were walking to a ditch somewhere to get stoned, and she was standing in her driveway with the movers moving boxes around her.

I had never seen such a beautiful girl. The sun glistened around her, and her hair blew in the wind in slow motion. I couldn't take my eyes off her. She looked my way, smiling, and waved. I melted. It was love at first sight.

I looked at her that day, thinking about something terrible happening, so I could swoop in and rescue her from some unknown threat, becoming her hero. She would collapse into my arms in gratitude, and we would make love until she was exhausted and satisfied. I spent a lot of time in the shower thinking about her.

She was a year older than me, and I would stand at my locker looking at her, trying to get the courage to ask her out. Every time I started my trek towards her, my heart pounded out of my chest. I always chickened out, looked at her, nodded, and smiled as I walked by.

Oh my God, I thought, *she got to see me embarrass myself again.* I shook her from my mind and walked to the bar, chatting with one of the waitresses and ordering a glass of ice water. As I turned to walk back to the band table, Rachel stood in front of me.

"Looks like the rock star thing's working out for you," she slurred seductively. I looked into her eyes, feeling tongue-tied and fantasizing about all the things I'd wanted to do to her since junior high school.

"Buy me a drink?"

I smiled and motioned to the bartender to bring her a drink. I explained to her that it was time for the next set to start and that it was nice to see her again. What I really said was probably incoherent babble, but to my surprise, she followed as I walked to the stage and sat at the band table.

As the band entertained the audience, I watched the waitress bring Rachel an endless stream of drinks. During the breaks, the two of us were hitting it off, and I didn't give her drinking much thought. At the end of the night, the bartender brought me my tab.

What the fuck is this? I thought as I looked at Rachel, who was almost passed out on my shoulder. I felt trapped. I swallowed hard and dug into my pocket to satisfy the amount owed. It was more than I would make the entire weekend.

Part of me wanted to scream and tell her she owed me for the tab I paid. Another part of me convinced myself it was my fault for not explaining to the bartender that I was purchasing her one drink only. Either way, it didn't matter. She was hammered and wanted me to take her home.

She leaned over the center console of my car and took hold of my arm. I leaned my body towards hers and rested my arm on the console so she could rest her head on my shoulder. Things were going a lot better than I expected.

When we walked through the front door of her home, things became steamy. We made out in the doorway, and she grabbed my hand, leading me to her bedroom. As we walked through the bedroom door, I pulled her closer, kissing her passionately and slipping off her shirt.

I leaned down, kissing her perfectly formed breasts. She turned off the light and led me to the bed. This was the greatest thing that had ever happened to me. I couldn't believe the hottest girl in school was about to have sex with me, and I just knew she was going to fuck like mink.

I had needed to pee since we entered the car, and even with my erection, I could feel my bladder wanting to explode. I think I actually felt my back teeth floating. I gently lifted myself up and walked into the bathroom. I relieved myself, smiled at my reflection in the mirror, and prepared for the most incredible night of my life.

When I returned, she was passed out. I lay next to her and kissed her on the neck, trying to wake her to no avail. I rolled her over so she was facing me and kissed her while caressing her breasts. She felt like a wet noodle in my arms. She was out, and it was obvious she wasn't going to wake up. I rolled over on my back, and she rolled on top of me with her head resting on my shoulder.

I was as hard as a rock and had two devils sitting on my shoulders. They went back and forth in my head about whether I should or shouldn't have my way with her. I mean, it was consensual up to that point, right?

She started snoring like a buzz saw, and I started losing my erection. I knew that not violating her was the right thing to do, but damn, the other devil had a convincing argument.

Rachel shook me from my slumber. "Wake up," she said, "Wake up."

I opened my eyes, wondering where I was, and looked into Rachel's beautiful eyes, falling in love again. "What's the matter? Is everything alright?'

"Get up," she demanded. "You have to go."

I was confused. Confrontation had never been my strength, and Grandma's screams echoed through my mind. Tossing off the covers, I walked into the bathroom to relieve myself. I pulled out the folded rectangle of paper from my pocket and opened it. My stash was almost gone. It was time to visit Shelly.

"Hey, you want a bump?" I yelled over the sound of a vacuum cleaner.

The vacuum cleaner turned off as I walked into the living room. The sounds of a band I needed to familiarize myself with filled the room and saturated my mind. "Who's this?"

"It's the Dixie Dregs," she said instinctively. "Why are you still here? I told you that you need to go!"

"What's the hurry? You want a bump before I go?"

Her eyes glazed over as she looked at me, contemplating whether she would throw me out or walk to the bathroom and do a line. Doing a line won.

We walked into the bathroom, and I tapped the last of my stash onto a mirror. "What's the rush?" I asked again, handing her the dollar bill I rolled to make a straw.

"My daughter will be here in thirty minutes, and I need time to clean up." She said, feeling she owed me an explanation.

Daughter? I thought as I snorted the small amount left on the mirror and licked it clean. She never mentioned having a kid. "Are you married?" I snuggled in next to her, hoping for a little morning delight.

"No, not married. Just a single mom, and I really don't want her to see you." Frustration reflected in her voice, and she pushed me away.

"Okay," I said through my pent-up frustration and newly formed condition of blue balls. I walked to the bed and slipped on my shoes. I walked to the record player and kneeled down, looking at the album cover, leaning against the table on which her turntable was sitting. "Can I stay for one more song?"

She stood beside me, taking the needle off the twelve-inch vinyl disc and handing it to me. "Put it in the sleeve and take it with you. I'll try to find you if you're playing next weekend." With that, she pushed me out the door.

I sat in my car, celebrating my good fortune, and looked at the album in my hand. Five guys were jumping from a plane, and the words *Free Fall* followed their path downward. On the far right were the words Dixie Dregs, written vertically.

Steve Morse and his jazz fusion creations would have a direct impact on how I played guitar for the rest of my life. He was so damn fast, and the band was so seasoned. My new idol was Steve Morse, and I aspired to be as good as he was.

The following weekend, we were playing in a pool hall. It was called Pool and Que or something like that. It had a small restaurant that served burgers, fries, pizza, snacks, beer, and wine. There was an area in front of the bar with five tables and chairs.

Two steps down was a floor, where ten pool tables filled the supermarket-sized building. The pool tables left enough room against the walls for tall round tables and two chairs per table.

They filled the empty space, holding ashtrays and giving the pool patrons a place where they could place beer, food, cigarettes, lighters, and anything else they didn't want in their pockets.

We moved two tables from the dining area to the lower section and combined the other three to form a single long table. It provided sufficient space for a small stage and dance floor.

We hauled in our gear and set it up. The long table we made from the three wasn't more than five feet from our microphones, and there was no room for us to move on our makeshift stage.

We placed the PA speakers on the lower level, blasting the pool area, and relied on the monitors for stage volume. The first set was slow, and no one danced. They were there to play pool, not to listen to music.

I walked back inside from a bump and a smoke break before the last set began, and sure as shit, Rachel was sitting there waiting for me. I sat next to her, and the waitress brought us a pitcher of beer.

She scooted closer to me, and I could see she was already three sheets to the wind. I was relieved we were playing at a beer joint. The tab couldn't get as out of control as it had the week before.

She drank the pitcher of beer I ordered during our break, and two more followed in the forty-five minutes it took to finish our last set. I watched from the stage, amazed at her drinking prowess.

It was Friday night and the first night of a two-night gig. It was also an eighteen-and-over club, so I was done and out the door by one-thirty. Rachel talked me into going to an after-hours club for a "quick" drink, and again, it cost more than I would make that weekend.

We headed to her house, and the previous weekend repeated. I thought I had learned from the week before and didn't get up to pee. But this time, as soon as her head hit the pillow, she was out. When she woke the following day, she shooed me out of the house again, and I didn't see her for another seven days.

The following weekend, she found me again, and I gave it one more try to see if she was interested in me or in drinking and hanging out with a band. I tried talking to her about getting together during the week, but it fell on deaf ears. When the bar tab came, my count went to three weekends, spending more than I made.

I was frustrated and had my answer. When we got back to Rachel's house, her shirt came off, and she led me to the bed, only to lie down and pass out again.

I loved playing with her titties, but there had to be more to this relationship than me buying her drinks and playing with them after she passed out.

I felt used. My childhood fantasies had been destroyed, and I was sexually and mentally frustrated. In my buzzed state of mind, I could only think of releasing my frustrations, anger, and disappointments. I unbuttoned my pants and beat off, leaving my man seed on her breasts. I walked out the door, and her life for what I hoped would be forever.

The following weekend, I informed the bartender that a lady might come in asking for her drinks to be put on my tab and that I wouldn't pay for them.

I didn't expect her to show up, so I did it out of precaution. I was surprised when she walked in the door. I watched from the stage as she approached the bar, and the bartender handed her a drink.

A conversation ensued, and she disgustedly dug money out of her purse to pay for the cocktail. She chugged down what she paid for, glared at me on the stage, and left. I never saw or heard from her again.

Another Brick in the Wall

1983 started with a bang, and the Internet was born when ARPANET adopted TCP/IP protocols, allowing data exchange among a network of different computer models. Quiet Riot found the commercial success that had eluded them for so long.

The Nintendo Entertainment System debuted in America, and in September, KISS shocked the world when they appeared on MTV without makeup, promoting a new video and album called *Lick It Up*.

A new branch of metal grew from the musical tree when Metallica released *Kill 'Em All* and Slayer released *Show No Mercy*, branding thrash metal into our psyche. Dimebag Darrell and Pantera released

Metal Magic, and Ronnie James Dio released his solo debut album, *Holy Diver*.

Ozzy Osbourne continued after Randy Rhoads' death with *Bark at the Moon,* showcasing Jake E Lee on guitar. Mötley Crüe hits its stride with *Shout at the Devil,* Iron Maiden releases *Piece of Mind,* and ZZ Top has its biggest-selling album, *Eliminator*.

Stevie Ray Vaughn brings blues licks back to the scene with his debut album, *Texas Flood*, and Thin Lizzy released their last album before breaking up, called *Thunder and Lightning*.

Bryan Adams released *Cuts Like a Knife*, Huey Lewis and the News released *Sports*, and Def Leppard released their most radio-friendly album to date with *Pyromania*.

After being on the air for eleven years and filming two hundred and fifty-six episodes, *M*A*S*H* aired its final episode. It was watched by more than 106 million viewers. The Stray Cats introduced us to rockabilly with *Rant N' Rave With the Stray Cats*. Madonna released her self-titled debut album, Cyndi Lauper released hers with *She's So Unusual*, and Culture Club began to dominate with its second album, *Colour By Numbers*.

Things were going well with Liam as we explored the new rock and metal of the day, learning popular songs of the day, and putting our own raw spin on them. We played at large clubs with stages, small clubs without stages, pool halls, frat and sorority parties, and NCO clubs on the military bases in the city where we lived.

Some of the sorority formal parties featured wardrobe malfunctions. The sight of bare breasts being revealed from a loose-fitting dress falling to a girl's waist always got my young male libido racing and my pants fitting a little tighter. During those times, I often wondered if I should have taken a different path and been the one enjoying the entertainment instead of providing it.

We were a working band and enjoyed all the perks that came with it. We worked every weekend, and nowhere was off-limits. If you had two hundred and fifty dollars to pay the band for the night, we were yours. Liam was a working machine. We never took a weekend off, and he booked as many Sunday afternoons as possible.

I was making a name for myself in the city and getting to know the local musicians. There were always wannabes and the occasional seasoned musicians in the audience, and since we were a party band, we welcomed all musicians to join us on stage for a jam session. The only caveat was that they had to bring their own guitars. No one was ever allowed to touch my guitars.

Bon Jovi, Ratt, and the Cult released their first albums in 1984. Whitesnake found commercial success with their album *Slide It In*, and Yngwie Malmsteen released his debut album, *Rising Force*.

The rockumentary *Spinal Tap* was released. Prince's movie *"Purple Rain"* and album of the same name entertained us and introduced us to his genius in rock and R&B.

The XIV Olympic Winter Games opened in Sarajevo, Yugoslavia, and five months later, the Summer Olympics opened in Los Angeles, California. Ratt had us going "Round and Round" with the release of *Out of the Cellar*, and the Scorpions rocked us like a hurricane with their ninth and most successful album to date, *Love at First Sting*.

Michael Jackson moonwalked for the first time, and Chrissie Hynde bounced back from losing two bandmates to drug overdoses, releasing her masterpiece *Learning to Crawl*. Talking Heads released *Stop Making Sense*, and Bruce Springsteen released one of the biggest-selling albums of all time, *Born In The U.S.A.*

U2 changed direction with *The Unforgettable Fire*. Van Halen released their sixth studio album, *1984*. Metallica again altered the direction of metal with their second album, *Ride the Lightning*. Bryan Adams released *Reckless*, and Stevie Ray Vaughan released *Couldn't Stand the Weather*.

A devastating blow also struck The Party Crew that year, and it would change my friend and lead singer, Liam, forever. It was just another gig. Just another biker bar. We played a lot of biker bars, and we liked playing them.

Bikers were fun, and they wanted to hear the music we were playing. They wanted to hear Steppenwolf, AC/DC, and the music that filled our set lists. They loved our band, and we would play New Year's Eve parties, birthday parties, and special events for their club.

During shows, the crowd would dance, play air guitar, yell, scream, and even punch each other in the face. Some sat on the stage, acting as a human buffer between us and the chaos. We were always protected, and I genuinely felt safe. On top of that, they had the best drugs, and they loved to share. They scared me, but I loved entertaining them.

Walking into the club that night seemed different from the other biker bars we had played. They all had pool tables and a dance floor, and they all had pretty nice stages. Despite that, this one seemed too nice. Too preppy. To mainstream. Hard to explain, but something about it didn't resemble any of the other divey hangouts the bikers inhabited. Even the bathroom was cleaner and smelled better.

The dance floor was enormous, with tables and chairs sitting on the carpet behind it. As we entered the door, the bar sat before us, splitting the room in two. Ninety percent of it was on the dance floor side, and ten percent was on the other side of the wall. That side contained three pool tables, a few pinball machines, and a foosball table.

Liam greeted a friend he had invited to the gig as he and his girlfriend stepped onto the stage. She was dressed to the nines, had a killer body, and was beautiful. She was also visibly intoxicated, and the night was just getting started.

It was around eight-thirty, and we set up our equipment to begin the first set by nine. Five or six guys were in the back playing pool, but they didn't appear to be bikers. Harleys were parked in front of the club, but these riders didn't wear vests or patches.

I didn't give it much thought and expected to see the vested and patched bikers enter the door later that night. I concentrated on more important things, like finding a bathroom these guys wouldn't enter while I was performing my involuntary ceremony before the gig.

The girlfriend, as I now call her, made her rounds to the band members. She bent over, talking to me as I kneeled on the floor, plugging in my effects pedals. Her shirt hung down, exposing her small yet perfect and bare breasts. She looked down, noticed my view, and smiled, bending lower to make sure I could see everything.

I stood feeling uncomfortable, and she hugged me. She grabbed the back of my neck and kissed me. I pulled away, knowing her boyfriend was watching, and could feel myself getting hard. She made her way to John next, letting him know she was hot and ready to party.

Given another place and another time, I would have fucked the shit out of her, but John was happily married. Sometimes, his wife would come to the clubs and sing with us. We all liked her, and John was not interested in what was being shoved in his face.

After John snubbed "the girlfriend," the boyfriend seemed unhappy about the situation and how his date was handling herself. The air thickened, and you could see his body tense. She became more flippant and rebellious with every word he used to criticize her.

Every problem I've ever seen happen in a bar had to do with a woman, and this woman was obviously out to cause a problem. Secretly, I prayed the club would remain empty and problems wouldn't begin.

Liam's friend and his girlfriend sat at the band table at the edge of the dance floor as we started playing. They were discussing and then stopped as the loud music overpowered their words. Things seemed to calm down as we got through the first set.

The unvested, unpatched bikers sat in the back pool area, dancing and playing pool. They would periodically walk to the back of the room, pool cue in hand, and whoop their approval of the band.

At the beginning of the second set, I watched as "the girlfriend" wandered back into the game room area and started hanging on the pool players. Her low-hanging shirt exposed her breasts as she leaned on the pool table across from the one shooting the cue. Her flirtations became exaggerated by their interest, letting them know she was ready to party and that she could be had, not by one, but by all.

By the third set, it became apparent she had no idea what she'd gotten herself into. They started passing her around, kissing her and running their hands up and down her body as one handed her off to the next when it was their turn to play.

The boyfriend wandered into the pool area as they lay her out on the pool table, holding her down and preparing to pull a train. He tried to intervene and retrieve her, but the bikers stopped him. They found their party for the night, and they weren't going to give it up.

We broke into the song "Born to be Wild" as the exchange became heated, and fists flew. The boyfriend never stood a chance and tried to escape, making it to the dance floor.

"Get your motors running," Liam sang as we watched in horror at what was happening. "Head out on the highway." There was nothing we could do. The four of us didn't stand a chance against these guys, and it was over by the time we could react.

The bikers surrounded Liam's friend, kicking and punching him in the head. His girlfriend screamed with grief as two of them held her and continued running their hands up and down her body.

I have never felt so helpless or disgusted as we watched his blood run onto the dance floor. The punching and kicking continued in time to the beat we were determined not to miss. They took turns playing with the girlfriend and beating her boyfriend. They laughed and cheered each other on during the quick ordeal.

We should have intervened, but we were all in a state of shock. Maybe the distraction would have helped this man and his female companion. Then. Just like that. It was over.

"Born to be wi-ild," we sang as two of the bikers grabbed the boyfriend's lifeless body from the dance floor and dragged him to the door. They threw him onto the pavement and seemed pleased with their actions.

They returned to the pool area, playing with their prize and retrieving their belongings. They pulled her out the door unwillingly. I imagined to finish the deed. The horror she must have been enduring was inconceivable to me, and I felt a sense of guilt. I honestly don't know if they beat this poor soul to death or what happened to his girlfriend, but from where I was standing, it wasn't good.

We ran to the door after they left, but the boyfriend was gone, and there was no sign of the girlfriend or the men who had pulled her away. All that remained were bloodstains on the concrete walkway.

Back inside the bar, we ordered a beer and shots from the bartender. We sat silently, drinking and staring into oblivion. A glance passed between us before we returned to the stage, visibly shaken, to play our final set to an eerily empty club.

Liam never spoke about it again, and we didn't want to bring it up. He never told us if he knew what happened to his friend or to his friend's girlfriend, but something had changed. Liam had been playing this circuit for almost 15 years, and we watched as the life drained from him physically, mentally, and creatively.

His playing hit an all-time low, and we could not only see his depression, but we could feel it every time we walked into the rehearsal room. At times, he would stand and stare into the nothingness of his mind. At other times, he would be coherent.

Liam had booked gigs in advance, and being the consummate professional he was, he kept his word. We played those gigs with his dead eyes becoming more vacant with each club we entered.

Sometimes, he would babble into the mic. Sometimes, we had to improvise the songs around him as he would lose his train of thought and forget the words. Other times, he would wander off the stage into the cold, dark night, and we would find him sitting on the side of the building or next to the van, shivering from the cold.

Toward the end, he would sit and strum a D chord repeatedly with no rhythm or time. It was sad watching his nervous breakdown occur, and it scared us all.

There was nothing we could do. We tried to talk to him. Tried to support what he was going through. But all we could see were his cold black eyes staring back at us.

Liam gave us a calendar of the gigs he had booked when he was coherent. We knew they had to be played with or without him, and after they were fulfilled, we went our separate ways.

Wicked Ways

Maybe the hair band craze started with Alice Cooper, who released their first album in 1969. Perhaps it began with the New York Dolls, who released their first album in 1973. Maybe it was due to Kiss, who released their first two albums in 1974.

Some might say it started to take off in 1975 when Randy Rhoads' band, Quiet Riot, served as the backup band for Van Halen at the Whisky À Go Go on the Sunset Strip.

However it started, there's no denying that the 1980s will always be remembered as the decade of hair metal. As the eighties progressed, the hairspray became thicker, and the hair got bigger, begging the question, "Who had the biggest hair?"

In 1985, the hair craze was everywhere. Mötley Crüe released *Theatre of Pain*. The Cult released *She Sells Sanctuary*. Dokken released their third album, *Under Lock and Key*. Ratt released *Out of the Cellar,* and Heart gained mainstream success with their self-titled album.

The supergroup USA for Africa recorded "We Are the World." "New York, New York," written and performed by Gerard Kenny, became the official anthem of New York City. John Cougar Mellencamp released *Scarecrow*, and John Fogerty, of Creedence Clearwater Revival fame, released his first album in nearly a decade, titled *Centerfield*.

Tom Petty and the Heartbreakers released *Southern Accents*. Phil Collins released "Sussudio," and Huey Lewis and the News released "The Power of Love." Michael Jordan was named NBA Rookie of the Year, and New York's Easter Parade was televised for the first time.

Dire Straits released their fifth studio album, *Brothers in Arms*. The Red Hot Chili Peppers released *Freaky Styley*. David Byrne and the Talking Heads released *Little Creatures*. INXS released *Listen Like Thieves*.

Whitney Houston released her self-titled debut album, which showcased the voice of a generation, and Weird Al Yankovic began his parodies of popular songs of the day with *Dare to Be Stupid*.

Metal continued to reign as Dio released *Sacred Heart*. AC/DC released *Fly On The Wall*, and Scorpions released *World Wide Live*.

Speed metal takes off with Metallica's first certified gold album, *Master of Puppets*. The lead guitarist and co-writer of several

Metallica songs, Dave Mustaine, forms Megadeth and released *Killing Is My Business...And Business is Good.*

Walt Disney World celebrates its two-hundred-millionth guest, and Microsoft releases Windows 1.0. The metal branch split when Exodus released its thrash metal album *Bonded by Blood,* and Slayer released their album *Hell Awaits.*

I moved on from being a laborer and found a new job where I didn't have to cut my hair, managing a record store. The memories of playing with The Party Crew felt more like a dream than reality, and both the good and bad experiences started to fade.

I don't think you ever process an experience like watching a man get beaten to death on the dance floor, and I would never listen to "Born to be Wild" the same again.

But with time, everything passes, and I eventually justified the experience by saying my eyes were open wide enough to see what the musician's life could bring. Thoughts of never playing again and living an ordinary life, if only briefly, crossed my mind.

Family meant more to me now, and I spent more time with Mark. He was fifteen and began seeking the same rock n' roll life I had. I could see the person he was growing into, and even though he was independent and spent little time at home, he looked to me for guidance.

I started teaching him how to play the guitar, and we would talk about life, girls, and how we envisioned our lives becoming one day. He practically lived in my house, and I never thought much about why he didn't want to go home. We would sit in the living room, doing bong hits, playing guitar, and working on his vocals and harmony guitar parts.

An old friend I grew up with came into the store where I worked, searching for a new yet obscure album by his favorite band. He had an older sister who was married and out of the house by the time we were eight, so I never got to know her.

She remembered me, though, and she knew I had been playing the clubs with The Party Crew. She wanted to see if I could come by and help her son with a band he was starting. They were all still in high school, and I agreed to stop by to see if I could do anything to help.

I pulled up outside their house and heard music as I got out of the car. They were set up in the basement, but the music still permeated through the walls.

I rang the doorbell, and after a few minutes, the music went quiet. The door opened, and a young man of about seventeen stood before me. He had long, blond hair that fell past his shoulders, and he smiled as he looked at me. "I'm Dustin," he stated. "I'm Gary's nephew."

We exchanged pleasantries, and he invited me in. I followed him down the stairs to the band room. Dustin, the boy who answered the door and was my friend's nephew, played the drums. Jake played the guitar, and Brian played the bass.

They were just a little older than Mark, and I soon learned they were all seventeen and eighteen. I excused myself to walk to my car and grab my equipment. They all volunteered to help, but I assured them there was a small amount and I would be okay carrying it myself.

I went to my car, did a quick line, and smoked part of a doobie. I grabbed the 50-watt practice amp I took to auditions and jam sessions, along with my bag containing my effects pedals, chords, and a tuner. The bag's strap slipped over my head, and I grabbed my guitar. The amp was heavy, but I could carry it with one hand.

When I returned, I set up, sprayed some Afrin in my nose, plugged in my guitar, and made sure we were all in tune. I started playing my favorite jam, a twelve-bar blues in A minor, and stood close to Jake and Brian so they could see my fret hand and follow the chords I was playing.

They quickly fell into the jam, and the rhythm section was strong enough for me to stretch out with some leads and experiment with playing the same chords they were now playing on different parts of the neck. They could play their instruments and maintain a steady groove.

Most importantly, they all possessed a maturity in life and music. I was pleased and impressed. They were into hair metal, and they knew about twenty songs. What they really needed was a lead guitarist and a singer.

It was a prodigious opportunity, and I was thrust into a singing role as we worked on vocal harmonies. These kids had more potential than I'd ever seen. This would have been an excellent chance for me to steer them into originals and make it big.

I thought about bringing Mark in to sing. He was two years younger than the youngest of these guys, but the difference between fifteen and seventeen is more significant than between eighteen and twenty.

I didn't feel his maturity level was where it needed to be for an opportunity of this magnitude. Also, we didn't have a PA, and buying one was cost-prohibitive.

My head still wasn't right after The Party Crew, and I didn't feel I had the same energy to go in the original direction, or if I was looking for a new project. I was still trying to process this career and find my way through it. Dragging a bunch of kids along on a journey I couldn't predict the end of couldn't end well, but my love of playing overrode my instincts, and I found myself showing up for every rehearsal and booking gigs for my new cover band.

The youngest in the band was still six months away from turning eighteen, so our options were limited to pool halls and eighteen-plus bars. Since the other members weren't much older, we picked up a few gigs, playing parties instrumentally, just as I had seen Phalanx do long ago. We also continued to jam and learn new songs in anticipation of playing the clubs.

A singer named Teddy joined the group soon after I started playing with them. He was a little older than the other three, but still younger than I was. He was obviously a rich kid who drove a new white Porsche. He also had his own sound system.

The problem was, he couldn't sing. Like many who aspired to be singers back then, he used his falsetto voice trying to reach the range of singers like Robert Plant and Geddy Lee.

He might have been okay if he had sung within his range, but his pitch was off, and his voice sounded horrible. I suppose that with time, he could have used his falsetto for screaming originals, but it just didn't work for other people's music.

The Four Seasons came out with their hit "Walk Like a Man" in 1963. When the Mikes and I heard it for the first time, our immediate reaction was, "Then sing like a man!" The Bee Gees also used their falsetto voice, but "Disco Sucked," and we made fun of them, too.

Teddy sucked, but the hard truth was he had a PA system, and we needed it to play out. None of us could afford one, so naturally, he was in the band, no matter his vocal prowess. We started recording ourselves so he could hear himself sing.

I'm not sure what we were trying to accomplish, but he would shrug off how bad his singing sounded and would not be deterred. On the positive side, I learned that recording everything was beneficial and a fast way to improve. It turned into a habit.

We finally convinced Teddy to adjust our song list to include songs within his range, and he continued practicing and learning new songs. The rest of us started sharing lead vocal duty and gave Teddy a tambourine to play when he wasn't singing.

We told him he could use his falsetto voice for the high harmonies, and he seemed content. We sounded good. Not as tight as The Party Crew, but after a few gigs and some harmony lessons for everyone, that would take care of itself.

We practiced together for probably six months when Dustin and the other original members made an announcement. One of them had a friend who was a manager at a roller skating rink. He gave him a tape of one of our rehearsals, and he asked if we could play an extended set during one of the skating sessions on a Friday night.

A roller skating rink. The thought bounced around in my head. I've played dive bars and pool halls, biker hangouts, and backyard parties, but playing a roller skating rink was never in my rock star dreams.

Liam had instilled in me that a gig is a gig. Even if it allows reality to slap you in the face and bring your ego back to Earth. The path to being a rock star is filled with venues, realities, and experiences you never could have imagined when you were fantasizing as a kid.

Childhood fantasies included images of playing in front of massive crowds that sang along and screamed your name. They adored the music so much that they committed the words to heart.

The narcissistic look through the eyes of an adoring crowd gives a false sense of ego to all who fall into its trap. Reality is never the same as fantasy, and reality includes roller skating rinks and shithole clubs.

The boys started getting hyped and excited as our debut night at the skating rink approached. They discussed the big night at rehearsals and had their own fantasies about how the night would unfold.

I listened to them, remembering I had felt the same way when I played my first gig. I wondered if any of them would suffer from throwing up and thought about the advice Liam had given me in case one of them did.

The night of the big event arrived, and I could never have foreseen the nightmare about to befall us. I don't remember if it was a one-hour or two-hour set, but I do remember that Murphy's Law set in, and anything that could go wrong did go wrong.

It was an evening gig, and skating had been going on all day. The stage was at the back of the building and was elevated, offering an unobstructed view of the skating floor. The only way to get to the stage was to haul our equipment across the skating floor and climb the stairs to the elevated platform.

Now imagine five long-haired, hair-sprayed, three-in-spandex pretty boys dodging skaters and trying not to damage the floor as we hauled Teddy's PA system and all our instruments across it. It took several trips, but we placed it all on its perch.

When I exited the bathroom after my pre-gig ritual of puking into the nearest shitter and doing a line, the band's energy was growing. Dustin sat behind his kit, and we all strapped on our instruments. The show was about to begin. I walked to the power amp and flipped it on.

This system was different from the tri-amp system we had with The Party Crew. It was smaller and didn't have lows, mids, and highs. It didn't have three different cabinets, and it didn't have a giant amp cabinet to haul around three different power amps and effects modules.

According to Teddy, it was the newest innovation in sound systems. It included a built-in power amp and effects, guaranteeing it would fill a room with Teddy's voice and our instruments. I flipped on the amp, and it turned off faster than it turned on. The fuse popped. Teddy pushed me out of the way, acting like it was my fault. He pulled another fuse from his pocket and inserted it into the socket.

It popped, too. After replacing it a couple of times and receiving the same result, he looked at me, and I could see a tear forming in his eye. His mouth started to move, but I couldn't hear his words over the music and sounds of the skaters.

I looked him in the teary eye. "Rock n' roll waits for no one," I yelled as I pulled a piece of gum from my pocket, unwrapped the aluminum foil, and placed the gum in my mouth.

I rolled the aluminum foil to the size of a fuse and shoved it in the hole, screwing the cap firmly in place. Visions of my amp smoking and the sickening smell of electronics burning screened in my mind. I wiped my running nose and flipped on the switch, holding my breath.

It worked, but when I put my nose close to the casing at the end of the night, I could faintly smell the burning electronics. It got us through the night, but wasn't going to go much further.

From our vantage point, I could watch the young girls go by, rubbernecking as they tried to get a better look at the young boys in the band. We had the look, and I was secretly a little jealous of them getting the attention. Based on the crowd's reaction, it was hard to tell how we went over, but the boys thought it was the best experience ever.

The local luthier and amp fix-it guy wasn't too pleased with me stuffing tin foil in Teddy's all-in-one PA. He was another sixties hippy guy, and he told me, in a laughing manner, that he would beat my ass if I brought him another one like that.

I apologized and wondered why these sixties hippie guys were all doing these back-line support jobs in the music industry. He charged me the fifty bucks I made playing the gig and another fifty out of my pocket. It was worth it. I still smile when I think of Teddy's face when I shoved that tin foil into his board.

That Smell

In 1986, Elvis Presley, James Brown, Little Richard, Fats Domino, Chuck Berry, Ray Charles, Sam Cooke, The Everly Brothers, Buddy Holly, and Jerry Lee Lewis were the first musicians inducted into the Rock N' Roll Hall of Fame.

Poison released their multi-platinum album *Look What the Cat Dragged In,* and Cinderella released their debut album, *Night Songs.* Ozzy Osbourne released his fourth solo album and began to find his identity. Queen released the unofficial soundtrack to the film *Highlander*. This would be their first recording released on CD.

Seventy-three seconds after liftoff from Cape Canaveral, the space shuttle Challenger exploded, killing all on board, and archaeologists found Tutankhamun's tomb in Egypt.

Steve Winwood was *Back in the High Life*, and the band Europe gave us the *Final Countdown*. The first anti-smoking ad featuring Yul Brynner aired on TV, and Geraldo Rivera opened Al Capone's vault, finding nothing.

Iron Maiden embraced technology and used guitar synthesizers on their sixth album, *Somewhere in Time*. Metallica released *Master of Puppets*. Megadeth released *Peace Sells... But Who's Buying*, Slayer released *Reign of Blood*, and Joe Satriani released his debut album *Not of This Earth*.

Halley's Comet made its closest approach to Earth. Chornobyl experienced one of the worst nuclear disasters in history, killing thirty-one and spewing radiation that reached the rest of Europe.

David Lee Roth left Van Halen to pursue a solo career. Van Halen released *5150* with their new singer, Sammy Hagar, a month before David Lee Roth's debut album named, *Eat' Em and Smile*.

Michael Jordan set the NBA playoff record with sixty-three points in a single game, and the Cleveland Browns became the first team in NFL history to have a play reviewed by instant replay.

Judas Priest released *Turbo*. Genesis released *Invisible Touch*, and Depeche Mode released *Celebration*. ABC broadcast The Oprah Winfrey Show for the first time nationally. Weird Al Yankovich continued his antics with *Polka Party*, and Mike Tyson became the youngest heavyweight champion in history at the age of twenty.

By the beginning of 1986, we were going strong, and my bandmates were turning into young men. We started building a following by playing at high school dances, parties, and pool halls. I even got us into LT's for a couple of weekend gigs.

During rehearsal, we discussed how a light show would help our stage presence, and a few days later, the original three introduced me to Ron. Ron was a pyrotechnic guy who had a large amount of stage lights and an ear for sound. He also loved to blow things up.

When I first met him, he had small scabs all over his face. I thought he was a methamphetamine addict and wanted to know more about him before allowing him near the boys in the band. Being the oldest, I felt it was my job to keep these guys safe and on the right path.

I had smoked meth before, and thought it was a horrible drug. I honestly believed meth would be the downfall of small American towns. I've had the unpleasant experience of people telling me they had cocaine, only to find out, too late, that it was meth. The burn as it enters the nasal cavity is excruciating, and it's a struggle to sleep or eat for days after.

In my opinion, nothing good ever came out of meth, and I didn't want a meth head working with electronics or explosives around me or the boys. When I looked at his hands and arms, they, too, had small scabs on them. People on meth like to pick at their faces and skin, leaving lesions and open sores, but his scabs were older and almost healed.

I asked him about the scabs, and he explained how he had taken a rock out of a stream and was heating it over an open fire when it exploded. The scabs on his face and arms were from small pieces of rock being blasted into his arms, hands, and face. He seemed proud of the shrapnel scars, and although I didn't believe the story, everyone thought he would bring an additional dimension to the band.

I relented, and we had him over to the band house. He worked his magic on our PA, and I had to agree. He had a golden ear. The sixth member of our band joined, and although our show got better, our pay became one-sixth less.

In 1985, John Cougar Mellencamp released the song "R.O.C.K. in the USA" on his album *Scarecrow*. We used it as our opener. It starts with a clean electric guitar playing an intro for sixteen bars. Then, heavy rhythm and lead guitars explode in, completing the intro before the vocals begin.

Ron wanted to start the night off with a literal explosion. He was reading "The Anarchist Cookbook." A book written by William Powell and released in 1971. In the book, Powell showed how to construct small explosives, such as flash pods, and listed all the necessary materials to create a blinding flash of light through a small explosion. Ron wanted to create these explosions on stage after the guitars came in on our opening song, and the boys agreed.

Ron never asked for more money, so I have no idea what the cost was to create this effect or where he got the materials. But every night, after I finished my pre-gig horror of losing my stomach and doing a line, I would get on stage, looking forward to an explosion going off next to me.

Two flash pods were set up on the stage, one on the right and one on the left. I could feel the heat and repercussions from the one set up next to me when they simultaneously exploded. They were almost tolerable when we played outside because they could be set further away. But when we were in a club, they would explode maybe two feet away from me and Jake.

With the addition of Ron, our following grew, and the clubs took notice. We no longer played the parties and were now strictly playing in pool halls, some of the local eighteen-plus clubs, and LT's was letting us play there regularly on Sunday afternoons.

I watched Liam book these clubs for a couple of years, and even though I didn't have access to his Rolodex, I knew how to put together a promo pack with a shit recording made during a rehearsal.

I was also fearless when it came to knocking on doors and getting our promotional pack into the hands of an owner or manager. Once people started following us, the rest took care of itself.

Bars are only concerned about the till or how much money they make. Having a following meant they would make money when we played. It also meant the clubs would invite us there to play more often. We had the following. We could fill a room, and we could fill a till. It felt good to be playing regularly again.

My ears rang after every gig from the cymbals crashing next to me. Now, I had a mini-explosion even closer, making them ring louder and longer. I hated it, and no matter how many times it happened or how hard I tried to brace for it, I was unable to prevent myself from tensing up and jumping when the explosion went off. To this day, when I hear the intro to that song, I still jump and wince.

Finally, the call came from LT's, and we landed the week-long gig we'd been waiting for. Working at the record store during the day and playing at night would be burning the candle at both ends, but it was only for a week. Getting this gig meant we made it. We were becoming rock stars, if only in our own little world.

The stage at LT's was big. Not as big as some of the flatbed trucks we played on during parties, but almost. As the lead guitarist, the left side of the stage, as viewed from the front, was mine. Dustin and his drums were in the middle at the back of the stage, and Jake and Brian were on the right side, with Brian and his amp closest to Dustin. Teddy was in front of Dustin's drums, and we all had microphones sprouting in front of us.

The first four nights went off without a hitch. Since it was a week-long gig, we didn't have to move our equipment. Every night, I would arrive at the club and chat up a waitress named Elle. The first time I met her, I stared at the nametag on her chest. "El? Ella? Ellie?" I asked.

"A-la," she said, stressing the long A on the first syllable and a short A on the second.

She told me she would never date anyone in a band and then became my lover. It didn't take her long to figure out what I was doing when my hands became clammy, I started sweating, and I excused myself to walk into the bathroom for my pre-gig warm-up.

When I emerged again, the boys would be on stage, tuning up. But tonight, one of them was missing. Jake, the other guitar player, was nowhere to be seen.

I walked up to Dustin and asked him what was going on. He said Jake wasn't feeling well and was sleeping in the van. I went out into the cold night and entered the van. He was covered up with a sleeping bag, shivering.

I thought about Liam and kneeled down, placing my hand on his forehead. He wasn't running a fever, so I assumed he was just exhausted. He opened his eyes as I touched his forehead. "I'm really tired," he moaned.

Shit, I thought as I looked at him, debating what to do. I have NEVER shared my drugs with anyone in any band I have ever played in. The only reason I was addicted to Afrin was that I didn't want anyone to know about my habit.

I had hidden it for a long time, and I hated the thought of everyone learning my secret. I wrestled with the idea for a while and thought now would be the time to break this rule. The show had to go on, or we would risk never playing here again.

I helped him sit up and pulled my stash from my pocket. "Here," I said as I laid out enough coke on the mirror for four jumbo-sized lines. I snorted two of them, handed him the mirror, and watched as he snorted the remaining two.

It took a few seconds, but his eyes opened, and he returned to looking like his old self. We jumped out of the van and headed into the club, where he chugged a beer and was handed another to take to the stage. We were late, but we got there.

There was just one problem. Nobody told me he was in the van sleeping because they had all taken Quaaludes earlier that day. The cocaine gave him a quick jolt, but the alcohol, boosted by the Quaaludes, quickly canceled the effects of the stimulant. Dustin counted off the intro of our opening song, and I could already see Jake staggering.

I prepared for the explosion, but it didn't occur. I looked at Ron and then at Jake, who stood over the flash pod, trying to see why it hadn't ignited.

"Move." I tried to yell as my body lurched towards his side of the stage.

The flash pod ignited, blowing its contents into his face. His hair ignited and billowed into smoke. The repercussion stood him up straight for a few seconds, and then he fell backward to the ground, still clutching his guitar.

Time seemed to stop as everyone watched, shocked and horrified. I tossed my guitar to the ground and raced to his side. I knelt beside him, placing my hand on his chest.

"Bring me a wet towel and some ice water," I screamed as he started to convulse. I couldn't tell how badly his face was burned because of the black chemical residue pasted there. But this was bad. This was really, really bad.

I snatched the towel from the ice water and pressed it to his face, trying to soothe the burn. My hands trembled as I wiped away the clinging residue, searching his skin for damage.

I scanned the room, desperate for Ron or anyone who could help. Elle kneeled beside me and held his hand as we waited for the ambulance. Ron was nowhere to be found.

I had let down not only Jake. I had also let myself and the band down. I blamed myself and would never shake the guilt. This rock star shit was becoming dangerous, and once again, I should have married Elle, accepted ordinary, and driven off into an ordinary sunset.

Jailhouse Rock

It's incredible to me how the human mind works. Even after I conspired against Teddy. Made him listen to himself sing. Blew up his power amp and expressed my feelings about his singing ability. He still wanted to be my friend.

I still thought he sucked as a singer, but we became friends and started hanging out. Sometimes, the meaner you are to someone, the longer they linger.

Maybe if I had been a dick to Rachel in the beginning and refused to buy her a drink, she would still be around. Doubtful, as it became apparent she was just an alcoholic who was looking for a cheap way to get drunk.

Rachel was five girlfriends ago, and Elle, the waitress from LT's, was now occupying my time. She was there with me. Helping heal my emotions and feelings of being responsible for Jake.

She was a fantastic lady, and I believe she loved me. Once again, I should have given up music and married her, yet something about being ordinary kept gnawing inside of me, and music was my only way out.

I had dreamed of attending the Musicians Institute in Los Angeles since I first heard about it. Teddy and I would talk about the school when we were out drinking and getting high. We both agreed that graduating from it would make us the monsters we had dreamed of becoming.

MI was a one-year school. Included within its walls were the Guitar Institute of Technology, the Bass Institute of Technology, the Percussion Institute of Technology, and the Vocal Institute of Technology. It was the closest to heaven that I'd ever be. One day in class, a future instructor of mine described it as a "great place to hide away and let your hair grow really long."

Teddy had a wealthy father who felt guilty about divorcing his mother. He was the ultimate "Disneyland Dad." If I was ever going to see the Guitar Institute of Technology dream come true, now was the time. So, when Teddy suggested we drive to Los Angeles to look at the school, I jumped at the chance.

I didn't have much money, but I didn't think it would be hard to get a grant or a loan for the small amount the school cost. I'd been saving money since working at the mall, so God willing, and the creek didn't rise too high, I could cover my expenses for a while. The stars seemed to align, and my future was shining bright. I would get my chance to break away from the ordinary.

After Jake returned home from the hospital, Teddy and I decided to take our road trip and check out the school. Jake's injuries weren't as serious as they looked at the club. His hair was gone, and the burns on his face were minor, second-degree burns that left limited scarring. He told us the scars would diminish with time. My guilt loosened. But the truth remained. It was my fault that it happened.

I continued saving money and even thought about giving up cigarettes and alcohol. But with my cocaine habit, it would have been impossible. Nothing's better after a line of coke than a cold beer and a smoke. I wasn't addicted to the booger sugar. I could give it up anytime I wanted. I just didn't want to.

In 1987, Guns N' Roses, which was comprised of two Los Angeles bands, LA Guns and Hollywood Rose, released their first studio album, *Appetite for Destruction*. Joe Satriani released one of his most successful albums, *Surfing With The Alien*, and continued to show his guitar virtuosity.

The Tracey Ullman Show premiered the first Simpsons cartoon, and Aretha Franklin was the first female inducted into the Rock and Roll Hall of Fame.

Smoking was banned in federal buildings. Michael Jackson attempted to buy the remains of The Elephant Man and released the follow-up to his smash album *Thriller* with *Bad*. Pink Floyd released *A Momentary Lapse of Reason*. Heart released *Bad Animals*, and the world population reached approximately five billion.

Bon Jovi released *Slippery When Wet*. It will become Billboard's top-selling album of the year. George Michael released *Faith*, and the single of the same name became Billboard's song of the year. Aerosmith released *Permanent Vacation*.

Whitney Houston followed up her debut album with *Whitney*. Def Leppard released their masterpiece *Hysteria*, and nineteen-year-old Zakk Wylde replaced Jake E Lee in Ozzy Osbourne's band.

Boy George was banned from a British TV show due to fears that he would be a bad influence on the audience. Britain performed a nuclear test at America's Nevada test site. The Butthole Surfers released *Locust Abortion Technician*. U2 released *The Joshua Tree*. INXS released *Kick*, and the birth of a galaxy was witnessed for the first time. R.E.M. told us, "It's The End Of The World As We Know It (And I Feel Fine)" with the release of their album *Document*.

The Pat Metheny Group released *Still Life*, and John Cougar Mellencamp released *The Lonesome Jubilee*. Anthrax gave us one of the best thrash metal albums ever recorded with *Among the Living*. The US stock market crashed, losing over twenty-two point five percent of its value in a single day. It would cause shock waves worldwide, with other markets losing as much as forty-five percent.

Our planning ended, and the day of our Los Angeles trip arrived. Greg had a Porsche with a new, state-of-the-art CD player that held five compact discs. We had a gram of blow and a quarter ounce of weed. For the occasion, Greg had splurged on a small "coke" kit, which included a mirror, a gold-colored razor blade, and a gold metal straw.

I got off work, finished packing, and did a couple of lines. We finally left around ten that night and headed west, going over the Rocky Mountains.

We'd been driving for almost twelve hours when we descended a mountain range, passing through a portion of Salt Lake City, Utah's city limits. I spotted a cop following us and slowed down, remaining as calm as possible. I woke Teddy as the red lights came on and the siren sang.

"Teddy, wake up," I half-whispered while shaking his leg.

He woke groggily, looking behind us at the cop car. He zipped up his new "coke kit" and placed it under his seat. We stopped on the highway's shoulder, and the police officer stopped behind us.

I remembered from my previous police encounter that he would want to see both our IDs. Since it was Teddy's car, I asked him for his driver's license, registration, and insurance papers.

Teddy dug them out of the glove compartment as the police officer walked to our car. I rolled down the window and produced the documents. He studied them, bent over, and peered into the car, looking over the top of his sunglasses.

There we were, two white boys in our late twenties who played in a band and dressed like we played in a band. Our hair was past our shoulders, teased and sprayed with hairspray so thick it wouldn't move in a hurricane.

To top it off, we were driving a new white Porsche. I've often wondered what that cop must have been thinking when he bent down and peered into our car.

"Where you boys headed today?" He asked as I looked at my reflection in his sunglasses.

"We're going to California to check out a music school," I replied sternly, trying to look him in the eye.

He looked at Teddy. "There anything in the car that I should know about?"

I watched Teddy's calm face contort as the policeman extended his gaze at him. He became tongue-tied, and I saw a tear forming in his eye.

Oh, Jesus Christ, I screamed in my head.

"There's a loaded gun in the back," Teddy screamed as he cracked under the pressure.

We were in serious trouble, and I knew it. "You've got a fucking loaded gun in the back, and you didn't tell me about it?" I screamed, thinking about the band house and why I moved out. "I've been driving all night with a loaded gun pointed at my fucking head? What the fuck is wrong with you?"

We quickly found ourselves sitting on the side of the road in our socks, with our snakeskin boots sitting next to us. We watched as the officer searched the car and our suitcases. He found Teddy's "coke kit" with our stash and half a joint in the ashtray.

Teddy whimpered on the roadside as the traffic whooshed by in front of us. I turned my attention to the police officer, trying to convince him of Teddy's father's great power and wealth. I was wired. I had driven all night. I was pissed off, and I might have been a little delirious.

The cop ignored my ranting, walked towards us, and asked Teddy to stand. He handcuffed him and led him to the car, placing him in the back seat. I expected to suffer the same fate as the officer walked towards me with a glaring look in his eye.

"I'm going to need you to put on your boots, get in that vehicle, and follow me to the police station," he barked. He wrote a ticket on his pad, tore it off, and handed it to me.

I jumped up and walked to the Porsche, checking that our belongings were still in place. I started the car and began a two-hour journey following the officer to the police station.

I never figured out why, but Teddy told the officer that the "coke kit" and cocaine were his. The cop gave me a three-hundred-dollar ticket for the half joint. Utah enforced strict weed laws at the time, but treated anything under an ounce as a misdemeanor.

Since I had half a joint, it was a low-grade crime, equal to a traffic infraction. Either that or I got lucky as hell. In a different time or place, I could have done twenty years for the small amount of pot he found.

The problem I now faced was that the cop took the half-joint and coke. There was nothing left to give me a boost. My eyelids were getting heavy, and I was feeling withdrawals from my habit. Looking at the back of the officer's car was hypnotizing me and putting me to sleep.

My Afrin supply was running low when we arrived at the police station. I parked, squeezed a spray into each nostril, and made my way inside. They were all interested in talking to me, and I continued weaving the tale of Teddy's father's importance.

I wove a very intricate tale about how Teddy's father would send his high-powered lawyers to invade this little outskirts town, and it wouldn't be pretty. I had no idea who his father was or how much money he had, but it seemed to work. After they processed Teddy for four hours, they released him, and we continued to Los Angeles.

Looking back, Teddy probably called his father as soon as they arrived at the police station. His father more than likely posted some kind of bond and promised Teddy would return for any court appearances. I'm sure the police laughed at me as I spun my wild tale, but I was still wired and feeling good about getting Greg out of this mess.

Walking in L.A.

After all the crap we went through to get there, Los Angeles was the biggest disappointment I had experienced in my life. Homeless people replaced the stars I had imagined would be walking the street. Some carried blankets, while others were picking through garbage cans outside the fast-food joints. It was dirty, and it looked like armed guards were standing outside McDonald's.

The Walk of Fame looked more like the Walk of Shame. We drove down Hollywood Boulevard and found a hotel to get some sleep. It felt like the life force was draining from my body. I needed a fix, and no matter how much Afrin I sprayed, it felt like cement was stuck in my nose.

I needed to find some nose candy and wanted to hit the clubs to find a score. Checking out the school could wait until tomorrow. Teddy wasn't feeling much like drinking after his legal ordeal, so I ventured onto the streets of Hollywood alone.

By the grace of God, I met a beauty in a bar who had connections to a dealer. Not only did I replenish my stash, but I got laid, too. The next day, I had a smile on my face, cocaine in my sinuses, and a fresh bottle of Afrin in my pocket.

The school was even better than I had imagined. One of the staff took us on a tour. It was full of people who looked just like us. They provided us with information on how to audition, and we left with a renewed sense of excitement.

We drove through the night to get back home. I tried to reassure Teddy that everything would be okay and that soon, we would be attending the school that would blast us into fame and fortune.

When we arrived home, I looked forward to sleeping for a couple of days, but my family was coming off the rails. Ken had left. Mom was in the hospital for an attempted suicide, and Mark was sitting in county jail for assaulting Ken.

In 1988, Calgary, Alberta, Canada, hosted the XV Winter Olympics, and Seoul, South Korea, hosted the XXIV Summer Olympics. Skidrow released their self-titled debut album, and Jane's Addiction released their debut album, Nothing's *Shocking*.

The Traveling Wilburys, consisting of George Harrison, Jeff Lynne, Bob Dylan, Roy Orbison, and Tom Petty, released their debut album *Traveling Wilburys Vol. 1*. Van Halen released *OU812*, Poison released *Open Up and Say AHH!*. Guns N' Roses released their second album, *Lies, and* Living Colour released *Vivid*.

Andy Gibb, a brother of the Bee Gees, died in Oxford, England, at the age of thirty. Robert Palmer released *Heavy Nova*, Lita Ford released her debut album *Lita,* and Melissa Etheridge released her self-titled album.

The movies *Big*, *Who Framed Roger Rabbit*, and *Die Hard* all premiered, and *E.T. The Extra-Terrestrial* was released to home video. Fourteen million copies had been pre-sold.

Metal was not to be outdone. Metallica released *...And Justice for All*, Queensryche released *Operation Mindcrime*, Soundgarden released *Ultramega OK*, and Slayer released *South of Heaven*.

The federal government enacted a smoking ban on domestic airline flights of two hours or less in duration. U2 released *Rattle and Hum*, and Sonic Youth released *Daydream Nation*.

Roy Orbison, after a four-decade career in music with twenty-two hits reaching the Billboard Top 40, died of a heart attack. He was fifty-two. One month later, his song "You Got It" reached number one.

I spent 1988 playing nursemaid to my mother and running her back and forth to the doctors to quell her depression. It turns out Ken wasn't such a great guy after all. He had been slapping my Mom and Mark around for years.

Mark grew tired of it and became big enough to do something about it. When Ken started slapping Mom, Mark beat the shit out of him. *Good for him*. I thought as the lawyer was explaining the story. Here was the problem. Mark was an adult and looking at serious time.

Mark's pent-up rage and anger must have been overwhelming as he fucked up Ken beyond all recognition. The lawyer told me that Mark broke Ken's cheekbones, knocked out some of his teeth, and cracked a couple of his ribs. He was still in the hospital.

They charged Mark with first-degree assault, a Class Three felony. If convicted, he would face a sentence of ten to thirty years. Ten years in prison for an eighteen-year-old was a lifetime, and I knew he wouldn't come back the same person he was when he went in.

Talking to Ken about dropping the charges was out of the question and, according to the lawyer, wouldn't matter even if he did. It was now in the district attorney's hands, and once they started the ball rolling, there was no stopping it.

After reviewing the case, the lawyer believed he could get the charges reduced to a Class Five felony. Because of the extenuating circumstances, he claimed he could prove it was a crime of passion. He said that he could get Mark off using self-defense as his argument.

Ultimately, he believed the DA would offer a plea deal before it went to court. *Everybody gets a fuckin plea deal, I* thought. It's built into our stupid system.

The public defender also suggested keeping Mark in school and making sure he graduated. "This would look good in the eyes of the judge," he said.

Even without this happening, I believed Mark needed to graduate from high school. I tried to divert his attention from what was happening and redirect it back to music. *We were both musicians, and the show had to go on* no matter what.

Fortunately for Mom, the house and car were in her name. That would be an additional court battle I didn't want to be around for. In the meantime, she went on welfare to support her and Mark and to pay what bills she could.

The sudden stress catapulted my drug addiction to new heights, and drinking became a nightly occurrence. The job at the mall I had planned on quitting was now a necessity. I had to pay what Mom couldn't, or we would lose everything. My dreams would have to wait.

Mark and I tried to carry on with musical interludes. Still, between his studies, his desire to hang out with his friends, lawyer visits, and my taking care of Mom, those were few and far between.

1988 was the worst year I've ever endured. My dreams of being a rock star were slowly fading, and my fear of being ordinary grew stronger every day.

In 1989, David Hasselhoff and Pamela Anderson ran along a beach as Baywatch was shown for the first time. Mötley Crüe continued their amazing run of metal songs with *Dr. Feelgood*. Mr. Big released their self-titled debut, and Joe Satriani released *Flying in a Blue Dream*.

Tesla released The Great Radio Controversy. Warrant released Dirty Rotten Filthy Stinking Rich, and The B-52s released Cosmic Thing, featuring "Love Shack."

Tiananmen Square in Beijing sees a million protesters, causing the Chinese leaders to declare martial law and move troops to the city. A Western photographer snaps a picture of a Chinese man standing in defiance at the front of a tank. The photo known as "Tank Man" would become one of the most iconic photos in history.

Phish released their debut album. Billy Squire released *Hear and Now*, and King's X released *Gretchen Goes to Nebraska*. The Berlin Wall was torn down, and East Germany opened its checkpoints for the first time in decades, allowing its citizens to travel to West Germany.

Soundgarden released *Louder Than Love*. Primus released *Suck On This*, and Soul Asylum released *Clam Dip and Other Delights*. Nintendo's portable video game system, the Game Boy, was available for the first time for eighty-nine dollars and ninety-nine cents.

Motorola introduced the world's smallest mobile phone, designed to fit in a shirt pocket. Its asking price was Three-thousand dollars. Tom Petty released *Full Moon Fever*. The Red Hot Chili Peppers released Mother's *Milk*, and Nine Inch Nails released *Pretty Hate Machine*.

The Simpsons' first season premieres, and network television pulls a Pepsi commercial featuring Madonna's "Like a Prayer" after widely publicized boycotts from religious groups. Nirvana released their debut album, *Bleach*. The hair band era was ending, and grunge was making its way onto the scene.

It's amazing how fast two years can go by when you're ass deep in drama. And with the end of 1988, 1989 promised to be a rebirth. Mom got back on her feet and started working again. Mark had his day in court, and the judge reduced the charges against him to a Class One misdemeanor. He was sentenced to six months in jail and a five-hundred-dollar fine.

I decided it was time to get my shit together and revive my dreams. I broke out the audition package I received when Teddy and I visited the Musicians Institute. I had been thinking about doing this for over a year, but with everything going on, I never found the time to open it. I placed the large envelope in my lap and carefully unsealed it, checking the contents.

The first thing that caught my eye was a cassette tape titled *The Monsters Are Here*. I slid it into my Walkman and put the headphones over my ears.

The first song by Joe Diorio was called "Like Someone In Love." It was a slow jazz number that was as awesome as the licks being played. As amazing a guitar player as he was. I just wasn't into jazz.

The second song from Robben Ford, "Imperial Strut," blew me away. I felt like a beginner again and wondered if I would ever be good enough to make it in this business.

The next was an introduction tape from Pat Hicks, one of the school's founders. "Hi, this is Pat Hicks." It began. "I'm recording this tape for the purpose of giving you some feeling of what goes on here at MI. The questions always come up. Are you a jazz school? Are you a Rock N' Roll school? Are you a school for studio musicians? And the answer is yes to all of that. We are a rock school, and we are a jazz school. And we are a studio musician school. In fact, you will be studying all aspects and styles of music here. And I'm pleased to say that you will be studying with some of the best in the business."

He went on to list some of the instructors and visiting faculty who had previously appeared at the school. I was in! I didn't need to hear anymore, but continued to listen anyway.

He explained that the school was open from nine a.m. to one a.m. daily and all day on Saturday and Sunday. At the end, he said he would appreciate it if I used the other side of the tape to play something. Anything that came to mind, so I could send it to them and they could figure out where I would fit in best.

I broke out my Fostex X-15 four-track cassette recorder and laid down a couple of blues progressions. After rewinding the tape, I recorded lead parts over them. Then I listened back, picked a few of the best thirty-second clips, and bounced them to a standard cassette."

I placed them in an envelope and, the next day, dropped it into the nearest mailbox. My heart pounded in anticipation as I walked away from the mailbox, patiently waiting for a reply.

When I finally received a reply, things seemed to be getting back to normal. Mark had been released from jail, and Mom was back to her partying ways. I couldn't tell if the six months in jail had made Mark a better criminal or if it had helped him be a more productive member of society, but it was good to have him home.

Mom went back to work, and it didn't take long for her friends to reappear in the house, turning the living room into their little party haven. The smell of marijuana and the sound of laughter filled the house once again. Everything was as it had always been, and all seemed well.

In anticipation of a successful audition, I applied for a loan and a grant before I sent the letter and demo tape to the Musicians Institute. Waiting for both was agonizing.

When I saw the letter from the MI sitting on the table, I picked it up and walked to my bedroom. I nervously opened the envelope and took out the letter, unfolding and reading it. A smile came to my mouth as I pumped my fist in the air. I GOT ACCEPTED!!

The loan and grant came in a few days later. Between the money I saved living at home with Mark and Mom and the loans and grants, I figured I could make it close to a year if I was careful.

If it started getting tight, I could find a job washing dishes or working as a laborer at a construction company. But for now, it was time to concentrate on my playing.

Teddy seemed to disappear off the face of the earth during my time of woe, and I resigned myself to making this trip alone. This time, I would bypass Utah and take the southern route through Arizona.

It would take longer to get there, but I didn't feel like tempting fate and repeating a route that almost ended in disaster. If I lost this chance, I would lose my dream forever. I wasn't taking any chances.

As time passed, the last thing on my list was breaking the news to Mark and Mom. I waited until the night before I split to break the news. If they had a bad reaction, I wouldn't have to justify myself, look at their tears for an extended period, or endure a long goodbye.

The day of my departure crept up faster than anticipated, and I found myself at the dinner table telling everyone my good news. Everyone seemed stunned, then lightened up, congratulating me and wishing me well.

Everyone except for Mark, who disappeared into his room. I sat outside his door for what must have been hours, trying to explain what this meant to me, but it seemed to fall on deaf ears.

I packed everything in my car early the next morning. Mark came to the car with tears in his eyes. He hugged me, told me he loved me, and wished me well.

I knew it would be hard on him, but I also knew I couldn't live my life being ordinary. I just knew something better was waiting for me. Something extraordinary, and I had to find it.

The Guitar Institute of Technology

In 1990, Alice in Chains released their debut album *Facelift*. The Black Crowes released their debut album, *Shake Your Money Maker*, and John Popper released his sensational, harmonica-fueled debut album, *Blues Traveler*. *Beverly Hills 90210* debuted on Fox, and Mariah Carey showed the world her breathtaking range and unique voice on her self-titled album.

Bo Jackson knows football and baseball, as he became the first athlete to be named to both the NFL and MLB All-Star Games. Douglas Wilder became the first African American to be elected governor of Virginia. Jon Bon Jovi released his debut album, *Blaze of*

Glory. It would reach number one on both the Billboard Hot 100 and the Album Rock Tracks chart.

Poison released their third album, *Flesh and Blood*, featuring two top hits, "Unskinny Bop" and "Something to Believe in." The album would reach number two on the Billboard charts.

Warren Haynes made his presence known on The Allman Brothers' tenth album, *Seven Turns*. *Law & Order* premiered on NBC, and *Twin Peaks* premiered on ABC. *Dances with Wolves* and *Ghost* were both released in theaters.

Living Colour released their second album, *Time's Up*. Depeche Mode released their seventh album, featuring "Personal Jesus," and ZZ Top released their last album, using the synthesizer-driven production style showcased on *Eliminator* and *Afterburner*. They would return to the band's blues roots on the aptly named album *Recycler*.

The IRS seized Willie Nelson's assets, and Washington, D.C.'s mayor, Marion Barry, was arrested on drug charges. Pantera, with guitarist Dimebag Darrell, released *Cowboys from Hell*. Soul Asylum released *And the Horse They Rode in On*. Queensryche released *Empire*. Slayer released *Seasons in the Abyss*, and Iron Maiden released their eighth album, *No Prayer for the Dying*.

Mikhail Gorbachev became the president of the Soviet Union, and George H.W. Bush ordered Operation Desert Shield in response to Iraq's invasion of Kuwait. The Damn Yankees, featuring Ted Nugent, Tommy Shaw, Jack Blades, and Michael Cartellone, released their debut album, *Damn Yankees*.

The Voyager 1 spacecraft took a photograph of the Earth from three point seven billion miles away. This photo would become known as *The Pale Blue Dot*. Warrant released their second album, *Cherry Pie*, and Jane's Addiction released their second album, *Ritual De Lo Habitual*. Ronny James Dio released his fifth album, and Heart released their tenth.

NASA placed the Hubble Space Telescope into orbit, and LL Cool J released his album *Momma Said Knock You Out*. On August 27th, Stevie Ray Vaughan died when his helicopter crashed in East Troy, Wisconsin, taking one of the greatest blues players of our time. He was thirty-five.

It's also the year I made it to Hollywood. I had been checking out places to live before I left, and the school helped me put out feelers for other musicians who would be attending. I ended up in an apartment with three other guitar players. It was a shithole that was a fifteen-minute walk to the school down Hollywood Boulevard.

My new roommates included Joe, Hans from Germany, and, surprisingly, another Mike. We were all long-haired, wide-eyed guitar players looking to make our mark and become known in Los Angeles.

We all got along and spoke about which of us would be the first to get a break and become famous. Everyone paid a hundred and fifty-dollars a month, and since all I brought was pillows and blankets, I slept on the floor for the first couple of weeks.

A weekend, a newspaper, and a garage sale later, I had a ten-dollar twin bed and slept like a king. Some of the others had odd chairs and coffee tables scattered around the house, and we all brought small TVs.

We still needed a couch, so we all sat on our guitar amps while we watched one of the small televisions in the living room. We noodled, almost in a trance, on our unplugged electric guitars as we stared at the tube. Secretly, we checked out each other's licks, trying to see who was the best.

During the first week of school, I walked around in awe. We started the day in our homeroom, where an Australian who loved to sniff the giant markers he used to write on the whiteboard would teach us Harmony and Theory. We sat in class holding our guitars, running scales, and noodling as he spoke. Imagine that. Twenty guitarists endlessly noodling in a room with unplugged electric guitars. It was a beautiful thing.

From Harmony and Theory, we might go to Chas Grasamke to learn the song "Salty Dog" using Travis picking. We could learn blues guitar from Keith Wyatt, classical guitar from David Oakes, country guitar from Steve Travato, or funk rhythm guitar from Dan Gilbert.

From there, it was off to learn the Joy of Picking with Nick Nolan, Modes with Graig Turner, Rock Licks with Russ Parish, Whammy and Tremolo Techniques, or melodic playing with Nick Nolan. Modern Guitarmanship with Paul Hanson, Frills for Thrills with Nick Nolan, or Eight-Finger Tapping with Roy Ashen.

Then it was off to David Oaks' Guitarmanship class. We went to Sid Jacobs for jazz guitar, Nick Nolan or Keith Wyatt for rock rhythm guitar, or Ron Benson's arranging class. Jennifer Baton, who had worked with Michael Jackson on his Thriller tour, was available for private lessons.

Tim Bogert from Vanilla Fudge and the album Beck, Bogert, and Appice was there for vocal instruction. Paul Gilbert was there for private lessons, and Carl Schroeder was there for composition.

We might listen to a free-form jazz band playing on stage in the lunchroom while eating lunch. Or, at night, we might see Paul Gilbert's Los Angeles copy band, The Electric Fence, or Carl Verheyen and his band play a set from their new album.

On special nights, Peter Frampton or John Entwistle would come in for a talk and allow the students to ask questions. Paul Gilbert allowed us to peek into his mind and gave us an intimate look at his playing and writing.

Our guest speakers included Howard Roberts, Tommy Tedesco, and Robben Ford. Gary Hoey gave an impromptu jam trying out his new Zoom 9000, and Pat Hicks gave us a meditation exercise that I believed would stop my throw-ups forever.

When they included the cassette tape labeled *The Monsters Are Here* in the audition pack, they weren't kidding. I was in guitar heaven, and I learned from them all. This was the most extraordinary year of my life.

Joe and Hans liked to drink beer but weren't much into drugs. Mike and I still enjoyed indulging in some ganja, and of course, I still had the habit I didn't want anyone to know about. One night, we ran out of weed, and some students at school told us we could score on Pico Boulevard.

I spent some time trying to find the girl who had hooked me up when Teddy and I drove here a year ago, but she never came back to the bar where I had found her. Deep down inside, I hoped I would find a new dealer for both my drugs of choice as we jumped into my old Pinto, unfolded the street map we could never fold back up, and headed south on N Highland Avenue.

From the I-110 South, we reached Pico Boulevard. We slowly scanned the area around us. It was rundown and looked like gangs could be hiding in every alley. It was scary. Hesitantly, we exited the car and looked at each other, hoping the other would say they didn't need to get high after all.

We trudged down the street, keeping an eye open for someone to help us score or any dangers that might be present. It was dusk outside, and we didn't want to spend any more time in this place than was necessary.

I was ready to tell Mike we should leave when a man of Latin descent walked past us. "Oh, two white boys walking down Pico Boulevard as it's getting dark," he mumbled as he walked by. "That's a good way to be killed." He turned, approaching us.

We froze, looking at him, gobsmacked. "So what's you need white boys, what's you need? I gots uppers. I gots downers, I gots what's you need, so what's you need white boys? What's you need?"

He opened his coat, revealing the inventory hanging inside. I quickly scanned for the fine white powder I would be jonesing for soon. I didn't see it. Mike stood as stunned as I, and together, we managed to squeak out "weed" while in my head, I was screaming cocaine.

He produced a small bag that might have contained an eighth of an ounce, opened his hand, and said, "Twenty dollars." He could have said a hundred dollars. As freaked out as we were, we wouldn't have argued.

We laid the money in his hand and heeded his warning. We ambled back to my car as quickly as possible, trying not to attract attention. When we were safely back on the freeway, we breathed a sigh of relief, laughed nervously, and drove home, anticipating the high we would soon experience.

When we arrived back at our room, we opened the bag, and it smelled like diesel fuel. Someone smuggled a brick inside a gas tank, and the bag wasn't airtight. We rolled a blunt and smoked it anyway.

It was shit, and the anticipation was the best part of this high. I was glad I hadn't scored any coke, and I would see if Mike wanted to hit the clubs with me the next day.

There was no way either of us would go back to that street to look for the dude we met, or anyone else, for that matter. We wondered if our "friends" at school had tried to pull a prank on us.

It was easy to find drugs at a club. Just look for a long-haired rocker with a spray bottle of Afrin stuck in his nose. They usually have connections for anything, and blow and grass were the easiest to score.

But for now, my adventures in the bars would have to wait. It was time to return to school and learn more from the monsters inhabiting the halls and classrooms.

Josh and Damien

In 1981, President Ronald Reagan deinstitutionalized the mentally ill and emptied psychiatric hospitals into "community clinics." These poor, confused people had nowhere to live and usually became homeless. The homeless problem skyrocketed throughout the country, especially in Los Angeles.

Smoking bans in America began in 1975 with the enactment of the Minnesota Clean Indoor Air Act. In 1985, Aspen, Colorado, became the first city to ban smoking in restaurants. In 1987, Beverly Hills followed suit, banning smoking in most restaurants, retail stores, and public meetings. San Luis Obispo would also ban smoking in bars and restaurants. But it would take almost twenty years before the rest of America followed suit.

Musicians Institute followed Beverly Hills' lead and banned smoking at the school. Those of us who smoked were sequestered to an area in front of the parking lot, in front of but across the street from the school's front entrance. We sat on a small rock wall that stood about three feet high, sucking smoke into our lungs while complaining about the smog in the city.

During one of our smoke breaks, a couple of guys and I were sitting on the wall smoking. A homeless guy was sitting a few feet away from us, bumming cigarettes and talking. One of our teachers walked down the street towards the school's front door. "I bet he has a color TV," the homeless man mumbled.

"What?" I asked, looking at him.

"Look how happy he is!" he responded louder. "I bet he has a color TV."

I watched the instructor enter the school, thinking about the profound statement the homeless man had just made. The homeless guy's vision of happiness was owning a color television.

My vision of happiness was becoming extraordinary. Other people's visions of happiness included amassing wealth and a collection of material things. Still others calculated their vision with power and influence. Very few were grateful for life and for what they had.

If he acquired the television, would he be happy? I thought. Or would he get caught in the trap of the ordinary, spending the rest of his life trying to become extraordinary? Sometimes, we find the happiness we seek within ourselves, not in the material things our world offers.

Meanwhile, the apartment I was living in was turning into a full-fledged band house. The partying continued nonstop, seven days a week, twenty-four hours a day. It was hard to sleep and almost impossible to study.

Girls hung out, waiting for us to become rock stars, hoping they would be the ones we were with when it happened. Some of them were amazing and would bring over groceries. Others would help us out financially. Still, others had connections to some of the best drugs in town.

All of them loved to fuck, and it didn't take long before my bed was full, and my booger sugar was back to overflowing. I loved living in a band house, but rock n' roll was for the young. Getting fucked up and laid all the time was cool and all, but I was twenty-eight, and it was a distraction from my destiny.

I still loved a perfectly rolled joint and the burn of a thick rail. But every time I looked at a pretty girl walking through the door, I envisioned a flashing detour sign pointed from the bottom of her neck to her crotch, beckoning me to give up my studies and spend the night in ecstasy and pleasure.

We were only a couple of months into the school year. I understood it was designed to make me feel behind, yet I knew I wasn't getting out of it what I should. My window of opportunity to succeed in this business was shrinking every day. I needed to find another place to live and study.

Up to this point, I had spent little money. If I found a new place for about the same price, I could still finish school before I needed to find a job. *Even if I had to find another job, I knew I would never be extraordinary living here.*

I started putting out feelers for a quieter place to live and suddenly found the school buzzing about a new student. George Lynch of Dokken fame was spending time at the school. Other students always surrounded him, so I never had a chance to meet or tell him how much I enjoyed his playing.

Part of me felt terrible for him. On one hand, I'm sure he enjoyed the attention and compliments from his fan base. On the other hand, he was there because he wanted to learn more about the career he was already successful in.

There comes a time in every guitar player's life when the joy of playing isn't enough. Hunting to find the right chord, the right note, the right groove is a fun stage of playing. But for those who have the ambition to be extraordinary, the desire to learn the whys and hows of music, as well as learning the instrument we choose to give our blood, sweat, and tears to, burns inside of us.

Even Randy Rhoads searched for classical guitar instructors while on the road with Ozzy. His thirst for knowledge was unquenchable, and his extraordinary licks were unrivaled. Unfortunately for George, his thirst would not be quenched at this school. His fame stopped him from getting the answers he deserved, and I only saw him in the halls for a few weeks.

After weeks of looking for a new place to live, my feelers paid off. I met Josh and Damien in the cafeteria while a free-form jazz band played on the stage behind us.

I must admit that I don't understand free-form jazz. The individual players all sound like they're playing in their own world.

Then they come back together in a coherent song, and then they're back in their own space, improvising again.

Josh was a drummer. Damien was a bass player. Damian was about my age. Josh was a few years younger. They were both from the same hometown in central California, were into metal, and had the look of the bands of the day. They were childhood friends who shared the dream of becoming rock stars. They had planned and saved for years before attending this school to ensure they could complete their studies without distractions. We had a lot in common.

Their house had two bedrooms, a living room, a dining room, a kitchen, and two bathrooms. We could hang a sheet in the dining room doorway to isolate it from the living room and create a bedroom. They were both on tight budgets, and their money was going faster than planned.

Living with them would cost twice what I paid at my new and out-of-control band house. I wouldn't be able to make it the rest of the year without getting a job. I explained my dilemma and told them I would let them know the next day.

When I went home that night, the never-ending party continued. Some of the school's European students started using our home as their hangout after Hans invited them to partake in the festivities. The party became increasingly violent as the year progressed.

I went into my bedroom to practice my lessons and was startled when I heard a crack in one of the walls and a couple of thuds on the floor. I flung open my door to an empty apartment with Hans and Joe lying on the floor, bleeding but coherent.

Soon, the police were at the door. I prayed they wouldn't search me and find the stash in my jeans pocket. This was the third time I'd been in the police's presence. I hated this scene and never wanted to be in their presence again.

I didn't want the fate I escaped with Ryan and the old band house to engulf me. The only way to change this destiny was to stay out of harm's way and away from any trouble that involved the police.

The officers moved their attention to Hans and Joe, and I asked if I could grab my guitar and go. They nodded their heads, and I was in my car driving down the road, heaving a sigh of relief and being thankful for dodging another bullet.

I decided then and there that I was going to get out of this house, regardless of whether I could afford it or not. The next day, Joe and Hans had white bandages around their heads from minor lacerations they had received in the fight the night before. I packed my car and informed them I was out of there and wouldn't be returning.

They looked at me with strung-out stares. I bid them farewell and jumped into my old Ford. I drove to the nearest pay phone, where I called Damien and Josh to inform them of my decision.

While in the Los Angeles band house, I got into the habit of wearing my guitar everywhere. I would brush my teeth with my right hand while my left hand was running Scales.

I would eat with my left hand while my right hand was doing picking and strength exercises. When I took a crap, I would work on my right-hand technique, including alternate picking, sweep picking, fingerpicking, and speed exercises.

I would eat, sleep, and shit guitar. The only time I took it off was during sex. Even then, the music would play in my head, or I would run scales in my mind. I was becoming the player I had always dreamed of becoming.

Josh's drums were set up in the living room, and televisions didn't exist in the house. We didn't need them. If we weren't working on new lessons we were given during the day, we were jamming and learning new songs. It was truly a match that couldn't be beat.

These guys had grown up together, and it seemed they could read each other's minds. Their rhythm section couldn't be touched, and my playing fit like the glove their freezing hand had been searching for.

Justin Sane

1991 started with American troops being deployed to Iraq, signaling the start of Operation Desert Storm. Aileen Wuornos became the first female serial killer when she confessed to murdering six men. Pearl Jam released their debut album, *Ten*.

The Smashing Pumpkins released their debut album, *Gish*, and the Spin Doctors released their debut, *Pocket Full of Kryptonite*. Queen released their last album, *Innuendo*, during Freddie Mercury's lifetime. He would die one day after announcing he had AIDS.

The Silence of the Lambs premiered. A ban prevented Dr. Jack Kevorkian from assisting in his parents' euthanasia, and four Los

Angeles police officers were caught on videotape beating a black motorist named Rodney King. The amateur footage is sent to a local news station. It rocks Los Angeles and the surrounding areas, leaving an uneasy feeling for any white person driving or walking on the streets.

Nirvana released their second album, *Nevermind*. It will sell eleven million copies in America alone. Brian Adams released *Waking Up the Neighbours*, and the single "Everything I Do" broke the world record by being number one for fifteen straight weeks on the UK Singles Charts. Hole, featuring Courtney Love, released their debut, *Pretty on the Inside*.

"Dances with Wolves" received the Oscar for Best Picture, and *the Super Nintendo* debuted in the United States, selling for two-hundred dollars. The Mighty Mighty Bosstones released their second album, *bringing horns back to rock*. Skid Row released their second album, *Slave to the Grind*, and Green Day released their second album, *Kerplunk*, featuring the smash hit "Welcome to Paradise."

Mass shootings and the term "Going Postal" shake the world as a former postal worker in New Jersey kills three people, including his supervisor and two of his co-workers. Another postal worker in Royal Oaks, Michigan, kills four and wounds five after being fired for insubordination.

A former alumnus of the University of Iowa shoots and kills three professors, a research assistant, and an administrator. He was upset because he did not receive an academic award.

The deadliest mass shooting in the United States before 2007 also occurred in 1991 when a gunman walked into a Luby's cafeteria in Killeen, Texas, killing twenty-three and wounding twenty-seven.

Metallica released *The Black Album*. Guns N' Roses released *Use Your Illusion I and II*. Ozzy Osbourne released *No More Tears*. Soundgarden released *Badmotorfinger*, and Primus released *Sailing the Seas of Cheese*.

The first website, info.cem.ch, was created, and a weather satellite documented a South Atlantic tropical cyclone for the first time. Bob Seeger and the Silver Bullet Band released *The Fire Inside*. France elects its first woman prime minister, and John Mellencamp finally sheds the name Cougar with the release of *Whenever We Wanted*.

Disney released *Beauty and the Beast*. Tom Petty and the Heartbreakers released Into The Great Wide Open, and researchers discovered the body of Ötzi the Iceman, believed to be from three thousand four hundred BCE to three thousand one hundred BCE, in the Italian Alps.

R.E.M. releases *Out of Time*. Magic Johnson tells the world he's HIV positive. The New York Giants beat the Buffalo Bills in Super Bowl XXV. Red Hot Chili Peppers released *Blood Sugar Sex Magik*. U2 released *Achtung Baby*, and a five point eight earthquake rocked the City of Sierra Madre in the Greater Los Angeles Area.

Motörhead released *1916*. Primal Scream released *Screamadelica*. Van Halen released their third album with Sammy Hagar titled *For Unlawful Carnal Knowledge*. It would debut at number one on the Billboard 200. Investigators found the remains of eleven men and boys in Jeffrey Dahmer's apartment. He will confess to murdering seventeen.

Damien, Josh, and I had been living and playing together for almost six months when 1991 began. We weren't just friends anymore. We were family. There were three months left in the school year, and we were all running short of funds. One of our new assignments was to play live on the lunchroom stage in front of the school.

We needed a vocalist. One who could do the assignment, be willing to learn songs, play in a cover band, and, most importantly, own a PA system. It took a while, but we finally settled on a guy from the Vocal Institute. His name was Justin. He seemed to fit in well, and we assumed his vocals were right on. The deciding factor was his PA system.

Our plan was to rehearse one song to perfection to ensure a good grade on our performance exam. Then, we would learn a night's worth of music and start playing the clubs before our money ran out.

After that, we could relax, work on originals, and live the life of rock stars. All plans contain a mixture of fantasy and reality, and this one had plenty of both.

Our first reality was that Justin never played a four-set night of cover material. That wasn't a problem in itself, but we didn't have any gigs lined up. I learned from Liam while playing in The Party Crew what I believe to be the first rule of being a musician. *If you have forever to put together four sets, it will take forever to put together four sets.*

The cart was before the horse, and it needed to be put in the right order. I was the only one who saw this as bad juju, and the only way I could fix it was to start booking gigs.

The biggest problem, and it was a personal one, was that Justin wanted to play "Born to be Wild" for the school performance. When he brought it up, I spit out a sip of water I had in my mouth.

I coughed the choke out of my throat and protested. "The song's too easy. We need something more complicated. Something that'll show our skill and virtuosity. Something that'll wow the teacher grading us."

Visions of Liam's friend lying on the floor, bleeding, and the faces of the bikers laughing and cheering each other on ran through my mind. I hated the memory of them running their hands up and down the screaming, grief-ridden girlfriend's body and tried to shake it. The band shut me down on all grounds, and I reluctantly agreed to play the song.

We agreed to convene at our house for our first rehearsal. I had played this song so many times that it had become a dark part of my soul that I didn't like to access. *We could do this in our sleep.* I complained to myself as Josh, Damien, and I practiced while waiting for Justin.

He would stand us up time and time again. When the stinging reality of being stood up finally hit us, we would take a break, smoke a joint, and talk shit about prima donna singers. We could sing the stupid song ourselves. I sang it in Wicked Ways, and Josh sang it in an old band of his, too.

However, we both hated our own voices, and we were focused on our instruments. We didn't want the distraction and couldn't pull off forty songs with the two of us singing them all. After the break, we would play some of the day's songs instrumentally, like I saw Phalanx do when I was in junior high school..

We had all but given up hope and set up one more rehearsal with Justin. We were working on some of the day's school lessons and moved on to some easy blues progressions on the scheduled day. I secretly hoped he wouldn't show and we would never have to play "Born to be Wild" again.

During a break, we heard a knock on the door. Justin stood in the doorway, a twelve-pack of beer in his hand and a bag of weed in his top pocket.

As singers go, Justin was the biggest prima donna I'd ever played with. He reminded me of the old joke. "Do you know how many singers it takes to change a lightbulb?" *Just one, but it takes the whole world revolving around him for it to happen.*

He was younger than the three of us, and it showed. He was about six feet tall, with long blonde hair and a lanky frame. Our project was due in two days, and if he hadn't shown up that night, we had resigned ourselves to the fact that Josh would sing "Born to be Wild" for our project. Then we would start the search for a new singer.

By the time we finished the doobie, he had drunk five beers and said he was ready to begin. We walked out to his van and helped him bring in the small section of his PA that he brought for the rehearsal.

When the PA was set up, and we were doing a mic check, the twelve-pack was almost gone. The last person I saw drink like this was Rachel, and I found it scary and impressive with both of them.

Justin believed we should have all the music learned before he arrived, so he could blow through it in one take and be on his way. His confidence exceeded his talent. He had a great voice. He just didn't have the experience, and I had a low tolerance for prima donna anything.

I've always believed embarrassment and humiliation are the best teachers, so we changed the song's arrangement. He looked confused as he tried to follow along.

He missed his cue twice and was feeling on tilt. It was hilarious. His face turned red as blood rushed to it, showing his embarrassment. He now had a choice. Quit or get his shit together and start showing up for practice. He had a fucking PA system, and I hated to lose that, but we had to make a stand.

I really needed to buy a sound system of my own to keep these posers and their drama away. That fantasy purchase went straight to the top of my "Things to Buy When I'm Famous" list.

Justin looked at us, and I could see the change on his face. He said he wanted to take a break to get his head together. He offered us a beer and walked to the next room, rolling a joint on the kitchen table. I hoped he would cut up a line, but he didn't.

I was a closet addict. If offered, I would do it. However, I wouldn't pull out my stash and expose my weakness. Instead, I put the Afrin bottle to my nose and inhaled the other substance I was addicted to. In the end, we went back to the original arrangement, and Justin sounded good.

I spent the next two days listening to Pat Hicks's meditation tape. "Begin to relax now. Let go"...The tape would start after the introduction... "You are no longer feeling any lax or limitations, any fears or doubts, and letting that power work for the good in your life... you're not worrying about how it turns out. You only know that it will be good and successful..."

It continued like this for about twenty minutes, and at the end, I would always add, "You won't feel the need to throw up before you get on stage." I just knew this would work, and I followed the tape's instructions to the letter.

On test day, I cleared my mind, breathed deep... and ran to the nearest bathroom, emptying my guts into the porcelain receptacle in front of me. After I cleaned my mouth and gargled with water, I suddenly felt the need for a line of my favorite sin. Pavlov's dogs came to my mind, and I giggled about how it works in humans, too. I stepped into the stall and locked the door behind me.

I've never been so nervous for a gig, before or since. I strapped on my guitar, still feeling like I wanted to throw up. The vision of watching Liam's friend get beaten was heavy on my mind.

Josh gave us a four-count, and the opening power E chord rang. We reached the second verse, and punches and kicks filled my thoughts. By the time we reached the lead part, the pool of blood forming on the dance floor stained my brain.

Before I knew it, the song was over, and I had no idea if I had played well, how we sounded, or how well Justin's voice sounded. There was no audience reaction, and everyone sat around eating and talking to one another, waiting for their turn. I thought I would have to wait until the grade came out.

The school, however, had state-of-the-art audio and video recording equipment. They handed us a VHS cassette tape of the performance and shuffled us into the cafeteria. I didn't care if I saw the performance or heard that song ever again. However, the rest of the band was excited to see it, so we pushed it into our VCR when we got home. The picture came on, and we sat in silence, carefully examining it.

Even at that time, it was a dated song. The editors at the school added some 1960s psychedelic special effects to spruce it up, and it helped give it a professional look. But it was still dated.

Justin's vocals were decent enough, but my playing was spot on. It took on a life of its own and deviated from the original. I was in shock and amazement as I pondered how a higher power could have taken control and produced something I couldn't have done alone.

Sometimes, I could feel this phenomenon when I was playing live. It would bring tears to my eyes, goosebumps to my skin, and calm to my mind as the music shone through my soul.

We solved the exam problem, and we received a passing grade. It was now time to address our financial situation. Justin agreed to sing with us if we could find gigs, and we went through LA looking for our next big show.

White Wedding

The Roxy, the Whisky a Go Go, and the Troubadour primarily featured original bands. Sometimes, they allowed cover bands to play if they met the metal criteria, but their policy of playing at their clubs was pay-to-play.

The band had to purchase a sizable number of tickets and then sell them to recoup the money spent. If the band sold enough tickets, they would break even. If the band sold all the tickets, they would make money.

The cold truth was that a brand-new cover band would lose money. The ultimate goal was to get into those clubs, but right now, we would be living on the streets if we didn't find a way to generate sme income.

Many clubs would cater to and pay cover bands to play the day's songs. *Gazarri's, The Central, and The Coconut Teaszer* were on the Sunset Strip. *Carlos' n Charlie's* was in West Hollywood. *At My Place* was in Santa Monica. And *Marty's On The Hill* was in the San Fernando Valley, to name a few.

Since we didn't have a name or a manager, none of these places would talk to us. When I entered the clubs and asked to see a manager or owner, bartenders typically greeted me, requested a demo tape, and promised to give it to the manager. We searched for a manager but found they didn't want to talk to us without a "buzz" around our name. It was an actual Catch-22 situation.

It took a while, but we found a new agent who was breaking into the business. He seemed to be a sleaze, but he had gigs, and they paid. The first gig was playing at the grand opening of a grocery store.

Now, think about that. A heavy metal band for the grand opening of a grocery store. This was even more soul-crushing than playing at the roller skating rink. However, there was one silver lining.

It paid two-hundred dollars a man and was a one-and-a-half-hour set. In clubs, my highest pay was one hundred and fifty dollars per person, and that was for a New Year's Eve gig. Our opportunity to begin the journey of becoming known and to pay our rent for another month had revealed itself. It just wasn't the way we had planned.

The day of the grocery store's grand opening was hot, and I mean fucking hot. There was a heat wave in Los Angeles that year, and the temperature didn't drop below a hundred degrees for weeks. The

1973 song "It Never Rains in Southern California" by Albert Hammond rang true, sure, and true.

We pulled in front of the grocery store, and Josh disappeared inside, reappearing with two orange extension cords. We set up our equipment on the blacktop in front of the store and blasted our speakers over the parking lot.

The blacktop absorbed the sun's rays and was at least twenty degrees hotter than the outside temperature because of it. It was almost unbearable. There wasn't even a canopy above us to shield us from the sun.

I walked into the air-conditioned store, my shirt soaked in sweat, searching for a bathroom. I shivered from the sudden temperature change as pterodactyls flew inside my stomach, and an urgency overcame me. It was time for my pre-gig ritual of throwing up and snorting a line.

The sun glared down on us as we played through our long set. A man exited the store with a little boy standing in the shopping cart. As they walked by and looked at us, the cart hit a bump. The kid did a front flip out of the cart, landing on the pavement.

Never taking his eyes off us, the father ran to his son's aid, returned the crying child to the wire cart, and disappeared to his car. Between songs, little kids ran up asking for autographs. You just can't make shit like this up, and I have to admit I found it all quite humorous, although I hoped the kid wasn't hurt.

When we were packing our equipment after the gig, the effects of throwing up and sweating were catching up with me. I started feeling faint and could feel a charley horse forming if I didn't eat a banana soon. The manager greeted us, wiped the sweat from his brow, and walked into the store.

He walked out of the store, paid us, gave us each a bottle of water, and told us we had earned our next gig. A wedding in Beverly Hills. I have to admit, for these being shit gigs, they paid well. This one was also two-hundred dollars per man. It would cover our rent for the following month. My outlook on these demoralizing gigs was quickly changing.

Justin's outlook must have changed, too. He started showing up for rehearsals on time. He did his homework by memorizing the lyrics to the new songs we were learning, and he stayed relatively sober for a few weeks to learn the arrangements of the new songs while keeping the old songs fresh in our heads.

We had a lot of work to do. The twenty songs we played at the grocery store needed to go to forty or more. Having The Beatles' song "Birthday" was always an excellent song to have up our sleeve if someone in the audience was celebrating their birthday. "Born to be Wild," we also kept up our sleeve because I refused to play it every night and hoped it would eventually be forgotten.

When we arrived at the Wedding Hall, the display of wealth was astonishing. I pulled up in my barely running and smoking Ford and stared at the building, fantasizing about the day it would be me with the wealth. Justin pulled up in his old van, carrying his PA and Josh's drums, and Damien and Josh pulled up in their old truck a few minutes later.

The security guards must have thought "The Beverly Hillbillies" had arrived, but were gracious enough to allow us to bring our equipment in through the front door.

This place was enormous. We walked through the main entrance, stepping into the welcome area that seemed to wrap around the building. A beautiful fountain set off to the side, standing about seven feet tall. It played its continuous symphony, giving off the relaxing sounds of running water.

There were three sets of double doors on the back wall. Each set of doors would reveal a vast hall that could be partitioned into three smaller halls. A giant stage was elevated in the back, and the room could easily have held a thousand people.

When we finished setting up our gear, the security guards had us move our cars to the back of the building and ushered us into the kitchen, where they hid us away with the rest of the staff. The chef made sandwiches for everyone except me. I never ate before a gig. I knew that in thirty minutes, I would be in the bathroom, heaving it back up during my disgusting pre-performance routine.

Justin seemed extra nervous that night, and the endless emptying of beer cans didn't concern me much, as I had watched him do it time and time again. Josh and Damien were enjoying their meal and became extra excited when I told them they could have mine.

Showtime arrived, and I walked out of the bathroom, joining the others as we stepped onto the stage, tuning up and getting ready for the show. These were all rich, preppy kids who obviously had a life of privilege. I wondered how they'd respond to our music, but they started dancing and enjoying themselves during the first set. It genuinely surprised me.

We started the night with older blues-based tunes from Cream, Clapton, Seeger, Mellencamp, and others. We gradually moved into heavier genres, such as Skynyrd, Sabbath, and Zeppelin. When the crowd, regardless of their musical taste, started feeling buzzed, and all music became acceptable, we would end the night with Metallica and Megadeth.

Drunk people are happy people when the music has a driving beat, and they can dance to it. No one remembers the songs that were played the day after the party. They only remember having fun and dancing with a hottie they almost got lucky with.

Justin began being a little wobbly during the first set, and I asked him to slow down until after the gig. We would all go in different directions during our breaks, so I had to trust that he would listen to my wishes.

I would find an empty stall in the bathroom to sit in and cut up a line. Afterward, I would head outside for a smoke. Josh and Damien would go do what they did, and I didn't even think about what Justin did during his breaks. Until he showed up noticeably late.

A couple of squirts of Afrin as I was leaving the stage would unclog my nose by the time I hit the stall. A fresh line of coke would open my nasal cavities further, and a couple more squirts of Afrin would finish the deed. The combination re-energized me, and I was able to breathe for at least another hour.

If we got lucky, we would all meet up before returning to the bar and smoke a joint. Something about being stoned and playing made the grooves so much groovier. The cocaine gave it the speed and hate prevalent in my style.

Everything was going well, and the crowd was digging us. Some of the younger crowd would come to our table to tell us what a great band we were. Others would walk to the stage to request a song that, if we knew it, we would be more than happy to play it. We ended our second set and took a break.

I started feeling relaxed and better about the gig, but I was worried about Justin being late again or not showing up at all. I thought about playing at everyone's weddings in the room and watched the money pile up in my mind.

A commotion began in the welcome area as I stepped on the stage to tune my guitars for the third set. I could hear girls screaming and men yelling in horror.

I rushed to the welcome area to see what the pandemonium was about. Justin was lying unconscious on the fountain's edge with his face in the water. His vomit was being recycled as the water and vomit soup reached the top of the fountain, falling onto the layers below.

It was disgusting, and the smell was overpowering the entire room. Damien and Josh joined me, and we stood in shock, paralyzed. The crowd looked at us, screaming in unison.

"You ruined her wedding. We should have never agreed to let a white-trash band grace our presence. You will never work in this town again," and other insults that surprised me, coming from an upscale crowd.

I always thought rich folk were more civilized and less full of hate than the average people we played for. I quickly learned that just because you have money, it doesn't make you a good or kind person. Most times, it's quite the opposite. No matter your race, creed, color, or financial status, we're all just people with the same hate and anger inside us.

I panicked. We would be lucky to make it out of there with our lives, let alone our instruments. I grabbed my main axe and ran to the kitchen, trembling as I waited for our manager.

We could hear the sirens of an ambulance taking Justin to the hospital with what we thought was an acute case of alcohol poisoning. One thing was for sure. We weren't getting paid.

We sat in the kitchen for what seemed like an eternity. Finally, the police arrived, and our manager arrived soon after. The crowd thinned, and we silently broke down our equipment. The police watched as we loaded Justin's sound system into his van and our personal equipment into Damien and Josh's truck.

We wondered if Justin was okay and if they had put him in rehab. The thought of rehab, no matter what it was for, scared me. I often wondered about the horrors Justin was sure to be enduring. The manager told us he would give Justin back his PA and demanded we give him the keys, which we didn't have.

He wouldn't give us any further information. We hatched many conspiracy theories during the coming weeks, and surmised that the manager had stolen Justin's van and sound system, selling them to pay for the lawsuit he surely had to fight.

In the meantime, the manager ghosted us. He wouldn't take our calls, and we couldn't get past his secretary when we went to his office. He didn't even have the decency to tell us where Justin was or what had happened to him. There was no way to prove or disprove our theories or assumptions about the manager.

The incident caused more disaster than just ruining a lady's wedding. Our rent was coming due, and we had to pay it. After a lengthy discussion, it was determined that failure was not an option and that being rock stars was the only thing that mattered.

Josh started waiting tables, and Damien washed dishes at the same restaurant. I returned to being a laborer for a construction company. The work seemed more challenging than it did a few years ago, and my muscles ached for the first week. But I made good money. I had enough for my third of the rent, utilities, and food.

There was also enough to support the habit I had kept secret all these years, as well as a fridge full of beer. I told people that my Afrin addiction stemmed from a deviated septum. It kept them from asking why I used it so much or why my nose was perpetually clogged.

When I first moved in with Josh and Damien, I called Mom and Mark to give them my new phone number. I called occasionally to stay up to date with news from home and even shared the school's number with them.

No one had ever called. Until now. Josh startled me when he handed me the phone and told me my brother was on the line. Something was wrong with Mom was the first thing that went through my mind. "Is everything okay?" I asked.

He explained that his band had broken up. His girlfriend left, and he hated his job. Most of all, he was tired of fighting with the string of men Mom led in and out of her bedroom while searching for her new knight in shining armor to make her life whole again.

Mark would turn twenty-one at the end of the year, and it was time for him to come to Los Angeles and stay with me. We laughed when I told him what happened to Justin and that his timing was perfect because we needed a new vocalist.

My stories made him feel better and less nervous. We spoke for over an hour, catching up with each other and vowing to stay committed to continuing our quest to be extraordinary.

I asked about the PA system he used in his old band. I had told him long ago that a sound system was the most important tool he could have if he wanted to be a singer. He listened and bought the system his band had been using.

It wasn't a vast tri-amp system like what we used in the Party Crew or an all-in-one system like Teddy's in Wicked Ways. It was a system he had purchased piece by piece, and it was powerful enough to fill a small club. That's all we needed.

I told Josh and Damien about his situation and his unique voice. I mentioned it would be nice to have one more person working in the house who could pay his share of the rent, food, and utilities.

More importantly, I justified that he had a PA system. He was my brother, I over-explained, and he was already a part of the makeshift family we had become. They agreed, and I asked him to come to LA and move in with us.

There were a few days of calls from Mom. "You're taking him away from me," she would sob, "and I don't know what I'll do without him."

But, in the end, she reluctantly agreed that a move would be in his best interest. She knew she couldn't keep him there. Fighting and crying were her ways of showing that she loved and cared about him.

Giving in was her way of admitting it would also be in her best interest if he left. She could continue sleeping with every man she met, and Mark wouldn't have to watch or listen to it.

I think Mark had already packed his PA system, clothes, and belongings in the bed of his truck when Mom gave him her blessing. He covered everything with an old tarp, tied it down, secured it, and hit the road the same day. Neither of us liked long goodbyes, and no one enjoys listening to their mother cry, so he made his getaway as fast as he could.

He pulled in late the following afternoon. It was good to see him. I worried about him making the long drive alone, but the life he had led up to this point had made him street-smart, angry, and independent. He filled out physically and was turning into a handsome young man.

His voice was a little lower, his hair flowed past his shoulders, and his clothes, although not intentional, were rock n' roll. I hugged him as he stepped out of his truck. It was good to be with family again, and deep down inside, I felt relieved knowing I had someone who had my back.

We spent a few weeks getting him up to speed on our set list. There were at least sixty songs by this time, and he would sit on the couch listening to his Walkman and writing down the words when we weren't rehearsing or going out on the town. We asked if there were any songs he wanted or didn't want to play, and added and subtracted accordingly.

We even experimented with some of the original material Mark and I had written long ago. Damien and Josh were impressed. I could see a new sense of vigor on their faces. This was going to work.

Josh's new, future ex-wife had a camera and enjoyed taking pictures. She took individual shots of each of us and group shots of the four of us posing and looking as bad and pretty as possible.

We recorded a week's worth of rehearsals with an old cassette player. Listened to each tape. Picked the four best songs and transferred them onto a demo tape.

We wrote bios for each of us and searched for a new management company. It was only a short time before one of the companies called with an offer to play at a New Year's Eve party.

Love Stick

In 1992, Americans elected Bill Clinton as the 42nd President of the United States. Muddy Waters won the Lifetime Achievement Award at the 34th annual Grammy Awards, and Blockbuster Video opened its first store.

Blind Melon released their self-titled debut album. Stone Temple Pilots released their debut album, *Core, and* the Gin Blossoms hit commercial success with their second album, *New Miserable Experience.*

Donna Summer received a star on the Hollywood Walk of Fame. Billy Idol was fined two thousand dollars for hitting a woman. *The*

Silence of the Lambs won the Best Picture Oscar, and Bruce Springsteen released *Human Touch* and *Lucky Town* on the same day.

Rage Against the Machine released their self-titled debut album, and Ugly Kid Joe hated everything about you with the release of their debut album, *America's Least Wanted*. Eric Clapton goes acoustic after the death of his son with *Unplugged*, and Neil Young does the same with *Harvest Moon*.

AT&T released a video telephone for One thousand four-hundred and ninety-nine dollars. Mike Tyson goes on trial for rape, and a jury of his peers finds him guilty. Barry Bonds signs the highest single-year contract in MLB history, totaling four point seven million dollars. Sinead O'Connor ripped up a photo of the Catholic Pope on Saturday Night Live. The Black Crowes released *The Southern Harmony and Musical Companion*, and R.E.M. released *Automatic for the People*.

Rage Against the Machine released its self-titled debut. Alice in Chains releases their second recorded disc with *Dirt*, and Damn Yankees follows suit with their sophomore release of *Don't Tread*. Weird Al Yankovic hit commercial success with "Smells Like Nirvana." Roseanne Barr-Arnold received a star on Hollywood's Walk of Fame. The Cartoon Cable Network premiered, and the XXV Olympic Games opened in Barcelona, Spain.

The year 1992 saw the sale of ten million mobile phones and the appointment of Jay Leno to replace Johnny Carson as the permanent host of The Tonight Show. Christopher Nolan released *Batman Begins*, and Spike Lee released *Malcolm X* in American movie theaters. Bon Jovi released their fifth album, *Keep the Faith*. Nirvana released their first compilation album, and after a five-year hiatus, Def Leppard released their fifth recording, *Adrenalize*.

Wembley Stadium hosted a concert in memory of Freddie Mercury. INXS released its eighth album, *Welcome to Wherever You Are, and* Sonic Youth did the same with *Dirty*. Roger Waters released his third solo album, *Amused to Death*. Disneyland opened in Paris, McDonald's opened its first restaurant in China, and three astronauts walked in space simultaneously for the first time.

The Cure releases their ninth album, *Wish*. Emerson, Lake, and Palmer released their tenth. The Ramones released their twelfth album, *Mondo Bizarro*. Santana released his seventeenth album, *Milagro,* and Fox began broadcasting on Wednesday nights.

Madonna's Erotica music video premiered on MTV, and eighteen days later, her book *Sex* went on sale. *Unforgiven*, directed by and starring Clint Eastwood, won Best Picture at the Academy Awards, and the Jerry Lewis twenty-seventh Muscular Dystrophy Telethon raised over forty-five million dollars.

Metal continued to rock as Soul Asylum gave us *Grave Dancers Union*. Black Sabbath gave us *Dehumanizer*. Iron Maiden brought *Fear of the Dark*. Megadeth had a *Countdown to Extinction*, and Pantera released *A Vulgar Display of Power*.

Two earthquakes rocked California. One earthquake measured seven point four on the Richter scale, making it the third strongest in America. Jeffrey Dahmer pleaded guilty to fifteen counts of first-degree murder, claiming insanity, and the US Marines landed in Somalia as part of Operation Restore Hope.

It was December 31st, 1991. We celebrated Mark's twenty-second birthday the week before, and my thirtieth birthday would be in eight days. We had been working hard since he arrived, and this new chapter of life promised us all great things.

The address the manager gave us for our first gig was in the San Fernando Valley. As we pulled up to the house, it was clear that this would not be a privileged white party, and our old, beat-up cars fit right in.

It looked like a lower-middle-class home with someone willing to shell out more than a thousand dollars for a live band. It sounded reasonable to me.

We walked to the door and were greeted by a man named Pedro. It was a Latin party, and I hoped they enjoyed the angry-white-boy music we played. Pedro assured me he had requested our music genre as he yelled something in Spanish to the guests who had arrived earlier. They walked to our cars, grabbed our equipment, and brought it in.

After setting up the equipment, Pedro invited us into his bedroom and laid out lines for us all. This was one of the best gigs I'd ever played. The audience dug us. The drugs flowed freely, and the beautiful girls were more than enticing.

Pedro kept a watchful eye on the girls as they danced in front of us like strippers in a club. I wanted to take two or three of them home for the night, but Pedro's stare and something inside me told me it would be an idea I would regret.

As the clock approached midnight, we began the customary countdown. We started the count at five, and everyone except Pedro rushed outside. He encouraged us to continue the countdown and stepped up to a microphone, joining us.

"Four. Three. Two. One." Guns blasted and echoed through the neighborhood as they fired their weapons into the night sky. We looked at each other, stunned. I mean, what goes up must come down, right?

Pedro could see that we were visibly shaken. "Just a tradition," he assured us.

Everyone rushed back inside, elated and reinvigorated from the gunfire and anticipation of the New Year. Marijuana smoke filled the room, and I wondered what kind of New Year's resolutions this group would be making.

The party raged around us as we followed Pedro to his room for another line. The rest of the night was more of the same, and just as his friends helped us bring our equipment in, they helped us take it back out.

We stood by the van as our new manager arrived almost on cue and walked to the house to greet Pedro. Things started getting tense, and after watching the gun show earlier, I didn't want to see the outcome of this altercation.

Our manager pulled out a contract, tapping the bottom of it. Pedro looked at me and then back at the manager. I shrugged, letting him know I had nothing to do with this part of the night. We would have played for the kindness and perks Pedro offered us. But business is business, and we were just whores that had performed a service. The pimps now wanted their cut, and emotion was only for the artistic.

I felt cheap and guilty as we watched Pedro disappear into the house. He reappeared and handed the manager an envelope. He looked at me again and disappeared back into the house.

The manager walked to our car, opened the envelope, removed his cut, and handed the envelope to me. "If I were you, I'd get out of here as fast as I could," he mumbled as he walked to his car. We heeded his warning and followed him out of the neighborhood.

The manager called about a week later. We had passed another of his trials, and he had a couple more parties for us to play. Depending on how we did, he wanted to put us on a bar circuit he and his partner had been booking for the past few years, up and down the San Joaquin Valley.

With the way the parties were paying, the thought of returning to the clubs for a quarter of the money didn't appeal to me. As much as the parties gave us all the illusion of being extraordinary, they were too few and too far between to support us. We didn't start this to be weekend warriors or, in this case, one-night standers.

It was January, and our next gig was a birthday party at a local college. It was a couple of weeks away. After that, we were booked for a Valentine's Day party at a different college. That one was more than a month away. I was tired of my labor job, and I knew Damien, Josh, and Mark were also tired of theirs. It was time to shit or get off the pot. We had to go all in.

It was typical Los Angeles winter weather, with nights dipping to forty and days reaching lows of sixty-five. It was light jacket weather, and I was a little taken aback when we pulled into the private and very Catholic Loyola Marymount University. We looked and felt out of place as we made our way to the recreation center, where we would be playing.

One of the students welcomed us, shaking our hands and introducing himself. He looked at our transportation and pointed to a parking lot a couple of blocks away, informing us that we should park there. He led us into the hall, where the night's festivities would take place.

I could feel Mark's anticipation as we lugged our equipment into the room. On our last trip, I scoped out the nearest bathroom, and we parked our cars in a hidden area of the parking lot, as the student ambassador had requested.

Mark's voice was the night's highlight. The college girls hung out at the front of the stage, staring at him and giggling with their friends. He had to be eating it up inside, but he was distant and seemed not to notice the attention he was receiving.

He seemed focused on a group of guys who had arrived late, looked out of place, and congregated in the back. During breaks, he disappeared outside. I imagined him wooing the girls and telling tall tales of his conquests in the music world.

Damien, Josh, and I were content hanging outside, smoking a joint, and chatting with some of the students about life at their school. I was always looking for a honey to take home, and would become more animated in my speech and actions whenever one happened by. After our break, I would slip into a bathroom, snort a couple of lines, and be back on stage before anyone noticed I was gone.

Unbeknownst to us were the music degrees offered at this school. The students studying guitar stood outside with us, complimenting me and picking my brain about my playing and the type of scales I was using. I've never been so thankful for the Guitar Institute of Technology and for learning Harmony and Theory as I was that night.

The Valentine's Day party went even better than the birthday party. We headed to California State University, Northridge, and found The Pub Sports Grill. It was a lot like the clubs I played in the Colorado circuit, but bigger.

There was a small, cramped stage, and they had moved the tables to make room for a dance floor. I'm sure the beer-stained floor and nicotine-caked walls had stories similar to those of the other bars I'd played. Although I'd bet they were classier stories.

As the students flooded through the doors, it became apparent that it was a semi-formal affair. Memories of the Sorority parties I had played in the past came to the top of my mind, and I stayed on the lookout for wardrobe malfunctions.

Walking onto the stage, I had an extra pep in my step. I anticipated continuing my never-ending quest to sleep with every woman I saw. Finding a Catholic honey. Ravishing her for the evening and adding another notch to my bedpost.

This time, Mark lit up as the pretty girls his age crowded the stage, and he became the night's focus. The drunker they got, the better we sounded, and the more the girls giggled and gazed at Mark lustfully. By the end of the night, Mark had hooked up with a casual crush and left with her.

This was the first girl I'd seen Mark hook up with, so Josh, Damien, and I humped all the gear to the trucks. We talked shit about prima donna singers and had a laugh as we made our trips in and out of the bar.

I felt good knowing that Mark was interested in girls, but I have to admit I was a little jealous and disappointed that my quest didn't produce my desired results. My ears rang as we headed home, silent and satisfied that we had given another outstanding performance.

We were building a name for ourselves, and the feedback we received was overwhelmingly positive. I imagined word of mouth would bring more gigs, but one-nighters were killer.

As much as I wasn't looking forward to the pay cut when we got on the road, I was looking forward to setting up and leaving our equipment for a weekend. The road was beckoning us, and our next stop was the bar circuit.

Turn the Page

The manager dropped off our itinerary, and we gathered around the table to see where the tour would take us, except for Mark. He was off with his new fling, and we only saw him for rehearsals. He never missed or was late to a rehearsal, so we were good with him being in love and spending time away.

The first run was going to be tough. Most of the clubs booked weekends or Thursday, Friday, and Saturday gigs. Some larger cities would offer live bands Tuesday through Sunday, but there was a lot of travel in between.

Compared with the parties, the pay sucked. The manager informed us that we would be paid fifty dollars per night plus fifty dollars a night for our accommodations. We would also get one meal daily from the club we were playing at and one drink per set.

"You can find hotels and motels for about thirty dollars a night," our manager explained. "I've set it up so there's minimal overlap between the gigs. If you all share one room, you should be able to cover your accommodations with the extra fifty a night."

He had a good relationship with the clubs. They sent him his cut and paid us our promised amount at the end of our stay. I'm sure he didn't want us to know his cut. And he certainly didn't want us to be paid the entire amount from the bar. He was probably afraid we would spend it on necessities or another room, so we didn't have to sleep two to a bed.

"This is just temporary," he continued. "You're not known, and it's hard to show what kind of crowd you can pull. The clubs will pay more once they know you can pull a crowd." He paused and looked at each of us. "From the feedback I've been getting from the shows I've booked for you, you'll be playing the bigger venues in no time. Then I'll be able to get you more money and get you an extra room."

The terms of this tour weren't in our favor, and I hated the idea of sleeping two to a bed. But I was thirty, Damien was twenty-nine, Josh was twenty-six, and Mark was the youngest at twenty-two. It was now or never.

Josh and Damien lived in a small town outside Merced. When we were close to their homes, they could stay with their parents or girlfriends, giving us a break from the tight quarters. They were even willing to take our remaining belongings from the house we currently lived in to their homes in Merced to store them.

We had two weeks to organize our affairs before hitting the road. Mark and I sold our cars and bought an old used van to haul the equipment. Josh and Damien would follow for the first leg of the trip and then drop their truck and our belongings off at their parents' home. We liked the fact that the manager wouldn't accompany or follow behind us to collect money. We didn't need an authority figure watching over us, and we damn sure didn't need a chaperone.

I kept his itinerary, list of cheap roach motels, and phone number safely in my guitar case. I hoped we would never need to call him, but knowing we could gave me some comfort.

We plotted our route on a large paper map that could be unfolded but never re-folded in the same way it was originally unfolded. The next afternoon, map in hand, we were on the road. Our first stop was Lancaster. From Los Angeles, it was about seventy miles. We took I-5 out of LA to CA-14 N, and about an hour and a half later, we arrived at our first club.

The place didn't surprise me when we walked in. It looked just like every other hole-in-the-wall I'd ever played. The stage wasn't the smallest I'd ever been on, but it was close. This stop would be for Friday and Saturday nights, so it was as good a place as any to begin. We unloaded the van, did a quick sound test, drove through a McDonald's, and set out to find a cheap hotel.

The motel cost us thirty dollars a night, and it should have been named Mildew Manor. It was about a ten-minute drive from the club, so we left Josh's truck in the parking lot. Mark wanted to stay behind and take a quick nap, so Josh threw him the keys, and I told him not to be late.

When we arrived at the club, I checked out where the bathroom was and did my pre-gig ritual of praying to the porcelain God above another piss-stained floor that smelled like shit. I stood up, dug into my pocket, and pulled out a folded piece of paper filled with the medicine to get me through the night.

I took part of the final paycheck I received as a laborer and invested it in an eight-ball before we left. I was trying to cut back, but who knew how long it might be before I could find a connection for more? Not having it before a gig, I believed, would be bad luck, if not disastrous.

I tapped a small amount on the small mirror I carried in my pocket and cut it up with my driver's license. I snorted half up one side of my nose and half up the other. Walking to the sink, I rinsed my mouth with water and checked my nose for any lingering powder.

I put my wet fingers in my nose and was still shaking and sweating as I exited the bathroom. I walked onto the stage, grabbed my guitar, and nervously tuned it again. I looked at my watch and raised my head to see an empty club with two waitresses and a bartender. It was almost time, and there was no sign of Mark.

I set down my guitar and walked to the band table. Josh and Damien were enjoying their first set drink, and their voices echoed in the open room as Mark walked through the door.

We performed to an empty club during our first set. By the beginning of the second set, people started filling up the chairs, and by the third set, the crowd loosened up, dancing and enjoying the night.

The first night went off with no major problems, and the four of us returned to the mildew manor that somehow smelled worse than the club.

When we arrived the following night, we were surprised to find the club packed. The waitress smiled, and the bartender nodded his head in approval as we mounted the stage to start our show.

The next stop was Bakersfield, about another hour and a half drive. We jumped back on CA-14 and headed north to CA-58, then turned west through the Tehachapi Mountains. As we traveled along the road, we could see wind turbines in the distance. It started to look and feel like home, minus the barren snow-capped peaks.

As we wound our way through the mountains, we caught a glimpse of a train going around a giant loop. From there, it was on CA-99, where we dropped into Bakersfield. I had my doubts about this city.

The Bakersfield sound was country, and I was concerned we would play behind chicken wire like the Blues Brothers did in the honky-tonk they played in the movie.

The van rides were long and monotonous, and Mark spent most of his time sleeping. This would be a Tuesday through Sunday afternoon gig. With the money we saved from our last hotel, we could afford an extra night, although sleeping in the van was sounding like a feasible option.

We walked into a more attractive club, a little bigger than average but still a beer-stained disaster. Some people were wearing cowboy boots and hats when we arrived, but the sound system was pushing out Mötley Crüe.

I chatted up a waitress, found the location of the puke chamber, and we went in search of a room. The rooms were more expensive in

Bakersfield. We wanted to stay close to the club, so instead of spending the day searching for an even worse Flea Haven Inn, we settled on the first and closest one we pulled into.

When we returned, the waitress had burgers ready for us. She was obviously pleased with her offering and had a big smile on her face when she surprised us with our plates of food.

I didn't have the heart to tell her I couldn't eat before a gig and would prefer mine after the first set, so I hesitantly forced it down, knowing it would end up in the crapper within the hour.

Tuesday night was slow, but by Friday, the bar was wall-to-wall people. The girls went where Mark and his voice were, and wherever girls go, boys are sure to follow.

After the show, the party continued in our motel room. Some of the local girls would follow us to our roach motel, where drugs, alcohol, and sex flowed freely.

The waitress became my flavor of the week. Although I liked to believe I was a one-woman man, the truth was I was promiscuous as hell. I would fuck anything, and the only thing I was looking for in a woman was if she would let me.

I think most boys my age shared the same moral substance as I did. Most of them didn't have the opportunity to live it out. I did, however, like my sex and drugs a little quieter and intimate, so instead of going back to the motel room with the boys, I spent most of the week at her place.

As Sunday rolled around, we piled everything into the van, said our goodbyes, and were back on CA-99 headed to Visalia for a quick Thursday, Friday, and Saturday night gig.

Visalia was approximately seventy miles from Bakersfield, and we could make it in under an hour. The temptation to stay the week with my new flame was there, but I said my goodbyes instead.

Damien and Josh's hometown was right outside of Merced. It was only a hundred miles further up the road than Visalia and a straight shot on CA-99.

We all decided it would be better to drive there and stay a few days to save money on our lodging. We could leave early Thursday morning and still have plenty of time to set up our equipment and be ready for the gig.

Mark and I stayed at Damien's parents' house, and it was peaceful. Damien's mom was the ultimate mother. She would cook for us and listen wide-eyed to the stories we would tell. I was a little envious, but happy for Damien to have been raised by such a wonderful lady.

I thought about me and Mark's mother getting high, partying with her friends, and bedding any man that would give her a smile. I fantasized about being raised by Damien's mom, wondering if I would have turned out differently.

After we left Damien and Josh's car at their parents' house, the cramped van revealed the realities and smells of a band on the road, even if only for a couple of hours at a time. When we arrived in Visalia, we all jumped out of the van and exaggeratedly breathed the fresh air. We walked into the bar, got set up, and I chatted up a waitress who was married.

I would have to find another girl to care for me for the weekend. As I walked into the bathroom to perform my nightly ceremony to the foul-smelling gods of porcelain, I noticed something had changed. The club was filling up, and it was only Thursday. We were earning a name for ourselves, and people were showing up, even on the off nights.

It was so busy on Friday that I had to sit in the stall and wait for one crowd to clear out and another to come in before I could exit. I didn't want anyone to know it was me puking my guts out.

When I walked out of the bathroom, I saw Mark hanging out with a group of guys that looked like the same group from Bakersfield. As I looked closer, I could have sworn they were also the same group he was hanging out with when we played Loyola Marymount University.

Bakersfield was seventy miles from Visalia, so they might have made the hour-long drive, but coming from Los Angeles would be a three-hour drive. That seemed unlikely. After a while, all audiences began to look the same. The stories were always a little different, but the faces began to blend. *Just a case of everyone looking similar*, I assured myself.

My thoughts quickly changed to how, with a large following, we could command more money and start playing more in the Los Angeles area. We could even throw in more originals and score the coveted record deal.

There were always lovelies in the crowds, and as it had the week before, the party continued in our room after the club closed. Some of the parties got pretty wild, and the women were only too eager to do whatever they thought necessary to be with the band.

Some were shared, and some were coveted, but in the end, they all got what they were after. A taste of fame. A night of being extraordinary. A chance to say, "I knew them when."

232

I hoped that the next time we were on this circuit, or possibly even on the return trip to LA, we would start making enough to get our own rooms. It wasn't so much the things we were doing in front of each other that bothered me, but sneaking into the bathroom every hour or so to do a line was tedious. I felt everyone was getting suspicious of my constant absence, but with the extracurricular activities going on, they probably didn't notice.

Sunday appeared. We loaded the van and headed back to CA-99, one of the most dangerous highways in California. Once on CA-99, we headed to Fresno for another Tuesday through Saturday gig. Fresno was only fifty miles from Visalia, and I was happy for the short drive.

We pulled into Fresno, and it was another ashtray with a liquor license. We jumped out of the cramped van, and I stretched my arms in the air, arching my back, yawning, and feeling fatigued from the road. We walked into the club in search of the bathroom.

We each ducked into a stall. I checked my stash, relieved myself, and took a little bump before walking out. Mark seemed busy in his stall, so I washed my hands, put my wet fingers in my nose, and walked out, spying Damien and Josh at the bar.

The three of us walked to the van and started hauling in the equipment, talking about how we wouldn't have to do this anymore when we were rich and famous. We got everything set up, and I was tuning my guitar when I realized I hadn't seen Mark since we arrived and hit the John. I wondered if he was out with one of his new girls somewhere, so I decided to check the last place I had seen him.

He was passed out in the bathroom stall. I freaked out a little and lightly slapped his face. "Wake up, Mark," I yelled. He breathed in deeply and exhaled slowly, still sleeping. I slapped him again, harder. "Wake up, you little fuck." He moaned and tried to open his eyes. I pulled him to his feet and walked him to the sink, splashing cold water on his face.

The color returned to his face, and he began to come to. He braced his arms on the counter so he could hold himself up, and I splashed more water on his face. He cupped his hand and rinsed his mouth with water from the tap. "What the fuck?" I asked, looking into his eyes.

"I don't know. I was just sitting there, and everything went black."

His eyes held a faraway look, and his pupils were dilated. I initially thought he was on something, and I attributed it to him just waking up. I pulled some cheap paper towels from the dispenser and handed them to him. "Well, when we get back to LA, the first thing we're going to do is get you to a doctor."

I waited for him to dry his face and put my arm around his shoulders as we walked out of the bathroom. We walked to the stage, ran through a soundcheck, and played a couple of the originals we'd been working on before the crowd arrived.

The crowd became energized, and the dance floor filled up as we played the second set. Mark was still different, and something seemed off. This had been going on since the Loyola gig. I couldn't put my finger on it, and he was sounding better than ever, but something was different.

I wrote it off as road fatigue and found myself sitting at the bar, chatting up one of the waitresses and watching the crowd as they flowed through the door. That's when I saw Mark's girlfriend from

California State walk in. He ran to her, gave her a huge hug and kiss, and walked her to our table.

I thought the week was going well. The waitress became my new special friend, took good care of me, and made sure I ate. Mark had his girl to hang with, and Josh and Damien told me he wasn't returning to the room after the gigs. I figured his girlfriend had rented a room, and the two of them were shacked up in it.

Then, the group of guys from Bakersfield reappeared, and they all knew Mark's girl. Something wasn't right, and I questioned the reality of the situation, wondering if the group was from Bakersfield or Los Angeles. *Why the hell would they travel this far?* I thought. I wanted to know who these people were.

My big brother instincts took over, and I followed them outside. They disappeared around the side of the building, and I crept to the corner of the dwelling, listening. I smelled skunkweed and heard a murmur of voices. I waited a few minutes, learning nothing, and headed back inside before Mark saw me, and it turned into a big deal.

Sunday rolled along too fast, and once again, we were loading our equipment and saying our goodbyes. Sometimes, I think the waitresses were as glad to see me go as I was to go.

Under the Bridge

Next, it was off to Merced for another Thursday, Friday, and Saturday show. I was excited to spend time with Damien's mom again and looked forward to the home cooking that only she could offer. I hoped the food and rest would do Mark some good, too, whatever condition he had.

On Tuesday, Mark and I decided to find a motel. As much as I loved Damiens's mother, I didn't want to inconvenience her more than we already had. I informed her of our decision during an amazing breakfast she made for us.

She insisted we stay, and as much as I hated to give up her cooking, I assured her we would be fine. I thanked her for the hospitality she had given us and then left. I wanted to give her a hug and tell her that I loved her and that I thought she was the greatest mom ever. Instead, Mark and I walked to the car in silence and drove off in search of a room.

That night, Mark and I holed up in the room, getting high, sleeping, and watching the tube. After that, we went to explore the small town and the club where we would be playing.

It was nice, just the two of us again. It had been a long time since we had a chance to catch up and get to know each other again. I felt the brothers were back and stronger than ever.

I came to this club with Josh and Damien before Mark arrived. They were feeling homesick and wanted to make the trip home to see their families. They invited me to come along, and I didn't feel like being alone, so I accepted.

Foghat played that weekend, and we stood on the second floor, watching them belt out their classics. It was a great few days and a well-deserved break from school.

Mark started feeling ill after we left Damien's parents' house, and by Thursday, he was running a fever and had muscle aches. I thought he was coming down with a cold, so I left him in the room while I met Josh and Damien at the club, and we started setting up for our show. This was one of the nicest clubs I'd ever played. Still a Skidrow Saloon, but a nicer Skidrow Saloon than the others.

It had a raised stage that sat about three feet above the dance floor, and it had an upstairs area, which was where we had watched Foghat the year before. On the far side of the upstairs was a game room with a pool table, pinball machines, and foosball tables. As we were setting up, I noticed flyers hung everywhere advertising a male strip show on Saturday night.

I drove back to the hotel to pick up Mark, who was still passed out in bed. When I woke him up, the fever seemed to have broke, but he was groggy, and his speech was a little slurred. I put him in the shower, and by the time he reemerged, he seemed like a new man.

On Thursday, we played to two waitresses and a bartender. On Friday, I went through my pre-gig ritual, and when I emerged from the bathroom, I was surprised to see the club was packed.

Damien and Josh's friends came out in support, and I spent the first fifteen minutes meeting and shaking hands with them. We turned the rest of the night into a wild party, shouting "Drink with the Band!" and "Somebody make some noise!" after almost every song.

Damien and Josh's friends sent up shot after shot, and after the first two, I asked the waitress to bring water or tea in my shot glasses. I informed her she was welcome to keep the cost of the drinks as her tip, and she smiled, obviously pleased with my statement. I thought I had an in. Then, she turned her back on me and wandered to the next table.

By the fourth set, I was amazed that Josh and Damien could still walk, let alone play. I'm sure we sounded worse than ever, but the party continued, and drinks continued to flow. At one point or another during the night, every drunk person in the bar came up and told us we were "the best fuckin band they had ever fuckin heard."

I'd heard it slurred through alcohol breath before, but I grew to hate it that night. Staying semi-sober and watching the drunken insanity was quite eye-opening. When the bar closed, we soon found ourselves at an after-party at one of Josh's friends' homes.

The next day, we all showed up at the club, hungover and looking like something the cat had dragged in. We were the only men allowed into the bar during the male strip show. None of us had ever seen a male strip show, and we all wanted to, so we made sure to be there before the show started.

We hung out upstairs for the most part, leaning over the rail and watching the ladies go wild as they shoved money down these buff guys' pants. I've been to strip clubs in the past, but men sit quietly, watching with their mouths open. Women, on the other hand, make a complete spectacle of themselves.

They hoop and holler, stand up and dance, and an endless supply of dollar bills seems to appear from their purses. It's amazing. Once the doors opened and the men poured in, plenty of guys were going to get laid. I planned to be one of them.

We walked down the stairs to the band table, where Damien and Josh had their girlfriends and friends sitting with them. Mark sat at the table writing something on a paper tablet, and I walked around the club, amazed at what was happening before me. I made my way to the bar to order a soda. And well, this is where my story began.

The first set ended, and Mark was still upset about our tiff earlier in the night. I was busy tracking down my fantasy for the evening and making arrangements for her to hang out and wait until after the show.

During the second set, the same group of guys from Bakersfield showed up and walked past the stage. Mark's honey was with them, too. It would have taken them at least two hours to get home from the Visalia gig and then another three hours to drive to Merced. *Who the fuck were these guys?*

Mark looked down as they walked by, smiling at his girl and nonchalantly nodding his head to the guys. He looked over at me and then into the audience. His angelic voice rang through the club, only to be broken by the sound of my screaming guitar.

During the second set break, Mark was out with his friends, and I was in the van smoking a joint and getting better acquainted with my new Latin lover. By the end of the third set, the crowd was thinning out. Mark's friends were upstairs playing pool, and my new future ex-wife sat in the front row, making me hornier every time I looked at her.

By the end of the fourth set, I didn't wait to say goodbye or put my guitars away. My one-night delight had her own apartment, and I wanted her so bad that I could have exploded in my pants just thinking about spending the night with her.

I informed Mark I wouldn't be staying in the hotel earlier and gave him the keys to the van, telling him to have a good night and not to party too hard. I figured some time alone with his girl and a good night's sleep would help him get over his anger towards me. Besides, I had my dick to think about, and at the time, he was much more important.

If the simile "She fucks like Mink" meant it was the best sex you ever had, then this lady was the most unique and expensive mink ever born. We literally fucked until the sun came up, and I have never felt more satisfied or content than I did with her.

I opened my eyes and looked at all her beauty lying next to me. She was even more beautiful that morning than she had been the night before. I fought the urge to go back to sleep and looked at the clock. It was almost eleven. We were supposed to meet at the bar and load the van at noon. I gave the new love of my life one more poke, and we headed back to the motel.

We pulled into the motel parking lot and started the usual make-out goodbyes. Every time I pulled away, I found myself locked onto her lips again. I didn't want to say goodbye, but it was getting late. She gave me her phone number and promised to come see us when we were playing in Modesto, which was about thirty minutes away.

My head was swimming as I watched her drive away, and I seriously considered giving up everything and marrying her. I had never met a woman so sensual, so beautiful, and so feminine in all my life. If Marilyn Monroe were reincarnated, it would be into this lady.

Mark was still sleeping, and the blankets entirely covered him as I opened the door and walked into the room, singing and celebrating my evening's conquest. I hadn't even thought about the fact that his girlfriend and friends from Bakersfield were nowhere to be seen. The room was empty and eerily quiet. Except for the hum of the air conditioner. The room felt cold enough to be inside a refrigerator.

I turned on the television. "Time to get up. You're sleeping the day away," I said as I turned off the air conditioner and walked past Mark's bed and into the bathroom. I turned on the shower and started to remove my clothes.

I could smell the new love of my life on my clothes, so I carefully folded them up and placed them on top of the toilet. *I will never wash this shirt again*, I thought as I jumped in the shower, allowing the water to warm my body.

241

When I finished, I wrapped a towel around my waist and searched for fresh underwear. "Come on, Mark," I raised my voice. We need to get to the club and tear down the equipment."

I returned to the bathroom, dried off, shaved, and put on deodorant. I winked at myself while pointing my thumb and forefinger at the mirror. "You good-looking son of a bitch. Don't you never die," I said as I shot my imaginary gun and smiled in celebration.

I walked out of the bathroom, grabbed Mark's foot, and shook him. "Come on, Bro, it's time to get up." I opened the curtains, feeling the heat from the sun. I grabbed his blankets and pulled them off, exposing his partially clothed body. A rubber hose was tied around his bicep, and a needle was stuck in the underside of his forearm. He was so pale that he looked like a zombie.

I ran to his side, grabbed the needle, and threw it across the room. I placed my ear against his chest and listened for a heartbeat. I pushed his stiff body onto its side and listened again. Nothing.

His backside was turning bluish-purple. His skin was cold but warmer than the room. I pushed him onto his back and started banging on his chest and performing mouth-to-mouth resuscitation.

I listened for his heartbeat again, and the tears started welling up in my eyes. I beat on his chest again and continued the mouth-to-mouth, crying and breathing hesitantly between my sobs.

Suddenly, the door opened, and Damien and Josh stood watching. "Please help me," I screamed through my tears, "Something's wrong with him, and we have to get him to a hospital."

I cradled him in my arms and tried to lift him from the bed. Damien grabbed the phone from the dresser under the television, and Josh sat next to me on the bed, helping to revive him and comforting me when he figured out it was too late.

I desperately continued beating on Mark's chest and administering my crude CPR. In between, I would cradle him in my arms and strain as I tried to lift him. I had to get him to the van so I could drive him to the hospital, but he was so heavy.

Sirens and red lights flashed and echoed in our parking area. I slumped into the corner, viewing the world as if in a dream, and wept in shock. *This isn't happening*, I thought as I watched the emergency responders lay Mark on a gurney and carry him out.

The officer's lips moved, but I couldn't hear what he was saying. I looked at Damien and then at the police officer he was talking to. The officer's words became clear, and I heard him say they had taken Mark to the General Hospital in the area.

I ran to the van, and Damien stopped me. "We've got to get our equipment from the club," he said, handing me his keys. "Take our car. We'll load up the van and meet you there."

I drove through tear-soaked eyes and spent my time in the waiting room, just as I had on the day Mark was born. I was angry and denounced God. I couldn't understand why he was doing this to us.

I had killed my brother, and I knew it was my fault. I felt riddled with guilt and changed tactics, this time trying to bargain with God. "Take me," I desperately cried. "Let him live and do with me as you will," I screamed in my head, hearing only silence.

Mark had overdosed on heroin and had been dead for at least twelve hours. I didn't even know he was doing heroin. The images of his girlfriend and the guys who first showed up at Loyola Marymount

University flashed through my mind. *Why didn't I see it?* I thought, *Why didn't I see it?*

"You didn't even try to help him," I screamed at everyone in the hospital, taking out my disgust with myself on them. "You didn't even try." I whimpered as I collapsed into a corner.

Josh and Damien arrived after loading our equipment at the bar and then unloading it at their house. They took me to Damien's parents' home, where I must have slept and cried for a week. Damiens' mom did what she could to nurse me back to health, and I knew I had to call my mom, but I wasn't ready.

When I finally accepted what had happened, I called her. She screamed between her sobs that God had taken the wrong son. It was my fault he was dead, and I should never have brought him to California. I knew everything she was saying was true, and her screams numbed me further.

Damien and Josh offered to take the money we made from our gigs and use it to have Mark cremated. We held a small ceremony in a cemetery outside of Josh and Damian's hometown.

Damian's mother was there for moral support, and I wished she had raised me and Mark. I started the long drive home with Mark's ashes in the only thing I could afford. A coffee can.

I had over twenty hours on the road to stare at the coffee can that represented the brother I once had and the blame I had placed on my shoulders.

In the end, my worst fears had come true. I had killed my brother, destroyed my mother, and would be imprisoned to live an ordinary life in an ordinary house in an ordinary town for the rest of my ordinary existence.